ARTICLE 370

ARTICLE 370

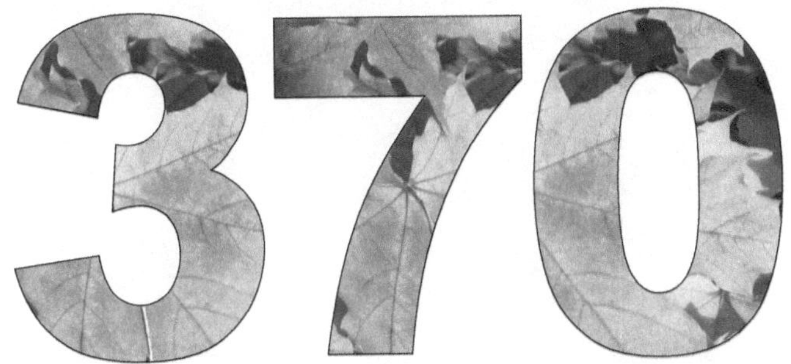

Explained for the Common Man

Sumit Dutt Majumder

PAPER MISSILE

NIYOGI BOOKS

Published by

NIYOGI BOOKS
Block D, Building No. 77,
Okhla Industrial Area, Phase-I,
New Delhi-110 020, INDIA
Tel: 91-11-26816301, 26818960
Email: niyogibooks@gmail.com
Website: www.niyogibooksindia.com

Text © Sumit Dutt Majumder

Editor: K.E. Priyamvada
Design: Shashi Bhushan Prasad

ISBN: 978-93-89136-43-2
Publication: 2020

Printed at: Niyogi Offset Pvt. Ltd., New Delhi, India

My father
Late Prof. S.M. Dutt Majumder,
an educationist,
who pioneered audiovisual education
in Assam

CONTENTS

PREFACE

With the Government's decision to do away with the special status of Kashmir provided by Article 370 of the Constitution of India, suddenly Article 370 became a household name, and everybody started talking about it—some well informed and others largely less informed or uniformed. From 5 August 2019, almost every day the news portals and the newspapers started putting up news reports and articles attempting to explain the issue, making some readers more enlightened while leaving a vast majority of readers bewildered. The moot point is that in order to understand the rationale behind putting Article 370 and Article 35A in the Constitution, as also the recent decisions of withdrawal of special status of Kashmir, one must have proper appreciation of not only Article 370 and Article 35A, but also the steps leading to their introduction and withdrawal. One must also know the basics of political and military history of Kashmir from the British Raj period and the events that unfolded from 1947 in the Kashmir Valley and the frontier areas of Gilgit, Baltistan, Kargil, Aksai Chin, etc.

Against this backdrop, Nirmal Kanti Bhattacharjee, former Director, National Book Trust and currently Editorial Director, Niyogi Books, asked me during the middle of August 2019, if

I could write a short monograph on Article 370, explaining the issues, the related events and views of the experts, for easy understanding by the common man. He referred to my previous book *GST Explained for the Common Man* published by Niyogi Books, and told me that the language, style and form for the proposed book could be as simple and readable as in my aforesaid book on GST.

It was quite a daunting task. First, the subject was outside my domain expertise and it was fairly complicated too. Of course, I have been following the news reports and articles, rather extensively on the developments in Kashmir, relating to the withdrawal of 'special status' of Kashmir. This was out of 'extra-curricular' interest on Kashmir that had developed in me after reading a book written by friend and batchmate, Ambassador Rajiv Dogra, *Where Borders Bleed*.

I may also mention, during my days in the Central Board of Excise and Customs, first as Member and thereafter as Chairman, I had the benefit of extensive exposition of the nuances of the Indian Constitution from Mr Pranab Mukherjee, then Finance Minister, while discussing issues related to taxation, particularly the GST Constitution Amendment Bill.

After mulling over it for a day, I decided to accept the challenging job proposed by Niyogi Books. My first act was to collect important books on the subject. My son, Rishi Majumder, a freelance journalist, gave me some books from his collection. Chittaranjan Bhavan at Chittaranjan Park, where I live, was very kind to let me use its library, a 'gold mine' for any reader. Jayanta Roy Chaudhury, a journalist of high repute who was also the General Secretary, Deshbandhu Chittaranjan

Memorial Society and Tapan Dhar, the Chief Librarian were very kind and helpful. Friends from various quarters helped by mailing or forwarding many articles and blogs relevant to the subject. My personal efforts also led me to many interesting articles and speeches. The articles were written by experts giving their views on withdrawal of special status for Kashmir—some, for the withdrawal and some against the mode of withdrawal; some against the withdrawal itself.

A few words about the book. Besides starting with a 'Prologue' and concluding with an 'Afterword', the book has five chapters. The 'Prologue' covers very briefly the background of events, starting from taking over of the affairs of India by the British Crown in 1858 till the framing of the Constitution of India in 1950.

Chapter I deals with the background to the Princely States during the British Raj and their final integration to India.

Chapter II deals exclusively with the Kashmir scenario. It covers the delayed accession of Kashmir to India by Maharaja Hari Singh and the conditions put by him in the Instrument of Accession. The military events and political developments in Kashmir, including Gilgit-Baltistan, Aksai Chin and Shaksgam Valley, that had a bearing on the introduction of Article 370 have been covered in this chapter. Indo-China border issues and the role of the UN have also been explained here.

Chapter III covers the events leading to the birth of Articles 370 and 35A, which stemmed from Article 370. This is a very important chapter of the book, inasmuch as it explains the reasons for insertion of Article 370, the process of framing it and its chequered history. It has also covered N. Gopalaswami

Ayyangar's Exposition of Article 370 (initially introduced as Article 306A) in the Constituent Assembly and the final impact of Article 370 read with Article 1. He was the Former Diwan of Kashmir, and later a Minister without portfolio looking after Kashmir matters in the Government of India. This chapter also covers the new Constituent Assembly for Kashmir, Sheikh Abdullah's rise and fall, introduction of Article 35A—its link with the Kashmir State Constitution, the Constitutional position of Kashmir in relation to India, before 5 August 2019, potential for problems with 'Special Provisions' for eight other states and the continuous dilution of Article 370 over the years.

Chapter IV starts with explaining the significance of Articles 370, 35A and 367. Thereafter it explains the momentous decisions of 5 and 6 August 2019, including reorganization of the State of J&K into two Union Territories. It also covers the Presidential Orders and two Resolutions by the Parliament. The effect on Article 35A of the Presidential Orders of August 2019 and the possibility of problems with special provisions for other states have also been discussed in this chapter.

Chapter V discusses the debates that started after the decisions of August 2019. It covers the views of experts on 16 different issues arising out of those decisions—some supporting the Government decisions and some opposing them. The experts whose views have been discussed include Soli Sorabjee and Mukul Rohatgi, both former Attorney Generals; Harish Salve, former Solicitor General; Justice (Retd) P.B. Sawant, former Supreme Court Judge; Senior Advocates like Rajeev Dhavan, A.G. Noorani, Gautam Bhatia, Gopal Sankaranarayanan and Faizan Mustafa, Vice-Chancellor, NALSAR Hyderabad.

The book concludes with an 'Afterword', which basically covers the developments in respect of various petitions before the Supreme Court. Considering that the Supreme Court has fixed the date for commencing the hearing by bunching all the petitions, the chapter concludes by stating that the jury is still out and the wait for hearing the last words from the Supreme Court has started.

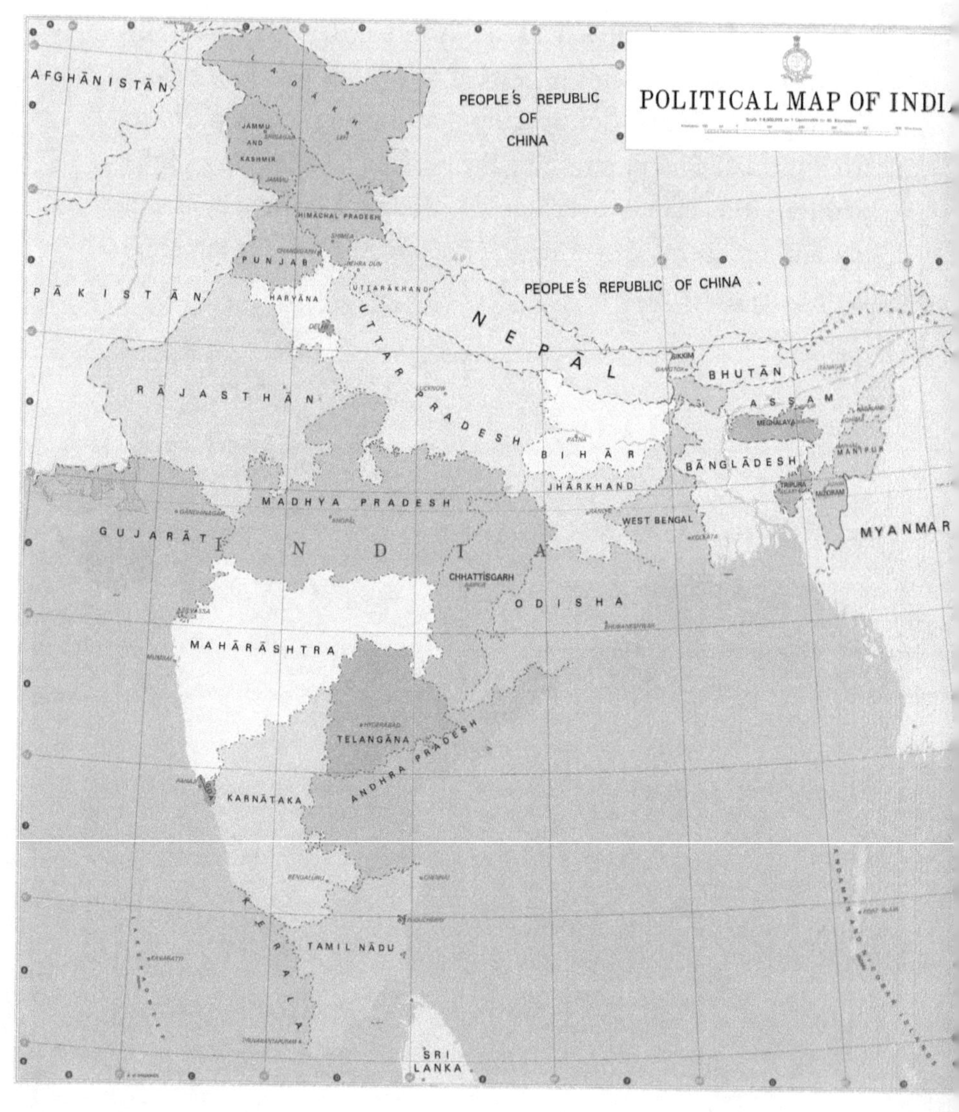

Political map of India issued by the Government of India in November 2019

Source: https://pib.gov.in/PressReleasePage.aspx?PRID=1590112

PROLOGUE

For about hundred years until 1858, large parts of the Indian subcontinent were ruled by the *British East India Company*. In 1858, one year after the *First Indian War of Independence*, also known as the *Sepoy Mutiny,* the *British Crown* assumed sovereignty over India from the said East India Company, and the British Parliament enacted the first statute for the governance of India under the direct rule of the British Government through the *Government of India Act, 1858*. This Act was guided by the principle of absolute imperial control without any popular participation in the administration of the country. The powers of the Crown were to be exercised by the *Secretary of State for India*, based in London, assisted by a Council of 15 members known as the *Council of India*. The Council was composed exclusively of people from England, some of whom were nominees of the Crown, while others were the representatives of the Directors of the East India Company. The Secretary of State, who was responsible to the British Parliament, governed India through the *Governor-General,* assisted by an *Executive Council,* which consisted of high officials of the Government. The administration of the country was not only unitary but rigidly centralized.

Princely States

Even when the British Crown assumed sovereignty over India from the East India Company in 1858, *there were around 565 Princely States* (referred to as *Indian States* in various documents), which were not annexed by the British Crown. The second largest and one of the most strategically important of these was Jammu & Kashmir. These Princely States were allowed to remain under the personal rule of their Princes or Nawabs or Nizam or Chiefs, under the *'suzerainty' of the Crown*. As against this, British India comprising the Provinces and certain directly administered areas was annexed by the British Crown.

Restricted reforms by the British Government

Some involvement of the Indian people in governance was brought in by the *Indian Councils Act of 1861* and the *Indian Councils Act of 1892.*

Slightly more effectively representative and popular elements were introduced by the *Indian Councils Act of 1909,* which was based on the reforms recommended by *Lord Morley,* the then Secretary of State for India and *Lord Minto,* the then Viceroy; these reforms were popularly known as *Morley-Minto Reforms of 1909.* However, this Act of 1909 *sowed the seeds of communalism* that ultimately led to the partition of country, by providing for the first time a separate representation of the Muslim Community. It may be recalled that the *Muslim League was formed as a political party in 1906.*

The *Government of India Act, 1915* was merely a consolidation of all the preceding legislations in its executive, legislative and judicial branches.

The Morley-Minto Reforms of 1909 had failed to satisfy the aspirations of the nationalists in India. Meanwhile, the *Indian National Congress, established in 1885,* which was under the control of the Moderates faced a challenge from its young and more aggressive members who wanted *self-government* during the beginning of the First World War in 1918. This was known as the *'Home Rule' movement.*

Government of India Act, 1919—first major reform

In this context, E.S. Montagu, the then Secretary of State for India, and Lord Chelmsford, the Governor General, came out with the *Montagu-Chelmsford Report,* which led to the enactment of the *Government of India Act, 1919.*

The Act brought about Dyarchy in the Provinces. It relaxed Central Control over the Provinces and the Indian provincial legislatures were made more representative. However, there were many glaring shortcomings, including the fact that the electorates were arranged on a communal basis. As World War I broke out, the Congress under the leadership of Mahatma Gandhi gave the call for *'Swaraj'* or *Self-Government,* independence from the British Raj, which was to be attained through *Non-Cooperation or the Satyagraha* movement.

Simon Commission—Communal Award

The *Simon Commission led by Sir John Simon* was sent in 1927 to enquire and report on the situation. Meanwhile, the British Government announced in 1929 that its goal was to give *Dominion Status to India.* The Simon Commission submitted its report in 1930. A Round Table Conference of all interested parties was called, *primarily to unite the Princely States with the British India Provinces under a federal scheme.* In 1932, Ramsay MacDonald, the British Prime Minister, announced the '*Communal Award*' which created separate electorates for Muslims, thus *creating further cleavage between Muslims and Hindus.* The *one-nation theory,* i.e. Hindus and Muslims constitute one nation, propounded by the Indian National Congress, led by Mahatma Gandhi and shared by Pandit Jawaharlal Nehru, Netaji Subhas Chandra Bose and Sardar Vallabhbhai Patel, got a setback. On the other hand, the two-nation theory, i.e. Hindus and Muslims are two different nations, propounded by the Muslim League, led by Mohammed Ali Jinnah, got a new lease of life.

Government of India Act, 1935—second major reform

Next, the *Government of India Act, 1935* was passed. It was the first time that the Act of 1935 prescribed a credible federation, taking the Provinces and the Princely States as units. But the *rulers of the Princely States did not give their consent for accession.* Thus, the Federation concept of 1935 was a reality only for the provincial Governments of British India but not for the Princely States. Further, certain good features of this Act of 1935, like a three-fold division in the Act—having a Federal List, Provincial List and Concurrent List—were later adopted, with necessary alterations, in the Constitution of independent India.

From the late 1930s, the national movement with demand for *Purna Swaraj,* i.e. complete *self-government* (Independence) started gathering momentum. It was clear that the Simon Commission, Round Table Conference and the four *Government of India Acts of 1909, 1915, 1919* and *1935* failed to satisfy the people's aspirations.

Independence Movement at a fast pace

In these circumstances, in 1938, *Pandit Jawaharlal Nehru* formulated his demand for the Constituent Assembly, without outside interference. This was reiterated by the Congress Working Committee in 1939.

In the context of Nehru's formulation, the Muslim League asserted its demand for the creation of a *separate Muslim State in the Muslim majority areas,* in the *Lahore Resolution* of 1940. The idea was later developed into the claim for dividing India into two independent states, and getting all the Muslim majority areas *including Princely States with Muslim majorities, such as Kashmir, included in that Muslim State.*

With the outbreak of World War II, when the war was at its peak and the Japanese and Indian National Army reached the doors of India at Manipur and Nagaland, the *Cripps Mission, led by Sir Stafford Cripps,* came to India in 1942 with a draft declaration on the proposal of the British Government relinquishing authority over India and the mode of handing over the authority to the Indian people. His proposal was rejected by both the Congress and Muslim League, for different reasons. Then, the Viceroy Lord Wavell held the *Simla Conference* in an attempt to make Muslim League and Congress agree. That also failed. The Muslim League was determined to have partition of India on communal lines. Meanwhile, the Congress under the leadership of Mahatma Gandhi launched the *Quit India* campaign in 1942.

Thereafter, the *Cabinet Delegation* was sent by England. In May 1946 they announced their proposal. Even as it rejected the claim for a separate Constituent Assembly and a separate State for the Muslims, it accepted many of the other critical proposals of the Muslim League.

Decision to Partition India

Finally, after some more negotiations, for the first time the *British Government accepted the Muslim League demand for two Constituent Assemblies and* two countries, in *H.M.G's Statement of 6 December 1946*. It was a big victory for the Muslim League.

H.M.G's next *Statement of February, 1947* included a promise that the British would certainly transfer authority, but it was not specified as to whom the authority would be transferred.

Mountbatten Plan

Next, Lord Mountbatten was sent as the Governor General in place of Lord Wavell. The *Mountbatten Plan* was given a formal shape by the *British Government* with a *Statement dated 3 June 1947*. The basic aim was to divide the country into *two Dominions—Muslim-majority Pakistan and India*. The British India provinces of Sind and Baluchistan were given to Pakistan. In respect of North West Frontier Province and the district of Sylhet in Assam, there was a referendum and people there voted for Pakistan. Similarly, West Punjab and East Bengal opted for Pakistan. The Dominion of India got the residuary territory of British India provinces.

The Mountbatten Plan having been carried out, the British Parliament came out with the *Indian Independence Act, 1947,* based on that Plan. This came into effect from *18 July 1947.* The Act provided that *from the 15 August 1947, there will be two independent dominions—India and Pakistan, and the Constituent Assembly of each Dominion would have unlimited power to frame and adopt any Constitution.* Thus, India became independent on the midnight of 14–15 August 1947, which Pandit Nehru famously termed as a 'tryst with destiny'.

Constitution in the making—interim arrangement

The next question was, what would be the structure of the Government in the interim, after attaining independence on 15 August 1947, pending the drawing up of a Constitution for independent India by the Constituent Assembly? To answer this question, the *Indian Independence Act of 1947, inter alia empowered the Governor General of India to adapt the Government of India Act of 1935 as the interim constitution till the enactment of a Constitution by the Constituent Assembly of India.* Thus, the *Government of India Act of 1935, as adapted, served as a Constitution from 15 August 1947 to the midnight of 25 January 1950.* The Constitution of India came into force on 26 January 1950.

Constituent Assembly

The net result of these legislations was that the previous Legislative Assembly and the Council of States ceased to exist from 15 August 1947, and from that day, the *Constituent Assembly,* whose primary job was to frame the Constitution, was itself to *function also as the Central Legislature of Indian Dominion*. In other words, the Constituent Assembly was to have a *dual function, constituent as well as legislative*. Thus, the sovereignty of the Dominion Legislature of India was complete.

The salient principles of the proposed new Constitution of independent India were first outlined in reports by various committees of the Constituent Assembly. The committees included *Union Powers Committee* led by *Pandit Jawaharlal Nehru, Committee on Fundamental Rights and Minorities* led by *Sardar Vallabhbhai Patel, Provincial Constitution Committee* also led by *Sardar* Patel, *Committee on Union Constitution* led by Pandit Nehru and *Steering Committee* led by Dr K.M. Munshi.

Constitution in place

On receipt of the reports, there was a general discussion in the Constituent Assembly, after which a *Drafting Committee* was appointed by the Constituent Assembly under the chairmanship of *Dr B.R. Ambedkar* on 29 August 1947. B.N. Rau, another luminary who was the Constitution Advisor, was one of the pillars in drafting the Constitution. The *Drafting Committee* embodied the decisions of the Constituent Assembly with alternatives and additional proposals in the form of a 'Draft *Constitution of India*' which was published in February 1948. After several sessions, the work was completed by the Constituent Assembly on *26 November 1949*, on which date the Constitution was passed.

The *provisions relating to citizenship, elections, provisional Parliament, temporary and transition provisions were given immediate effect from 26 November 1949*. The rest of the provisions in the Constitution came into force on 26 *January 1950,* and this date is referred to in the Constitution as the *Date of its commencement.* Accordingly, we celebrate *26 January* as our *Republic Day.*

Article 1(1) of our Constitution says 'India, that is Bharat, shall be a Union of States'. The full text of Article 1(1) reads as follows:

> **Article 1, Name and territory of the Union.**
> 1. India, that is Bharat, shall be a Union of States.
> 2. The States and the territories thereof shall be as specified in the First Schedule.
> 3. The territory of India shall comprise –
>   (a) the territories of the States;
>   (b) the Union Territories specified in the First Schedule; and
>   (c) such other territories as may be acquired.

It may be noted that India is not a 'federation of States'. Although the Indian Constitution is 'federal' in structure, the framers of the Constitution preferred the term 'Union'. *The Constitution of India was basically federal, but with strikingly unitary* features (Basu, 1997: 51). During the British Rule, India had a completely centralized unitary constitution until the Government of India Act of 1935. The Act of 1935 introduced the expression 'Federation of India' for the first time. In fact, our Constitution has basically continued the federal system, as explained in the Act of 1935.

MAP OF UT OF JAMMU & KASHMIR AND UT OF LADAKH

*Map of the Union Territories of Jammu & Kashmir and Ladakh issued
by the Government of India in November 2019*

Source: https://pib.gov.in/PressReleasePage.aspx?PRID=1590112

CHAPTER I

Background of the Princely States during the British Raj

From the early British times, the *Princely States in India, as* distinct from the Provinces in British India, had a *separate political identity.* At the time of the constitutional reforms leading to the Act of 1935, the geographical entity known as India was divided into two parts—*British India* and the *Princely States.* British India comprised nine Provinces and some other areas administered by the Government of India itself, somewhat like today's Union Territories; the Princely States comprised around 565 States which were mostly under the personal rule of the rulers such as the Princes, Nawabs, Nizams, etc. The Princely States were of different orders. Some States were under the rule of hereditary Chiefs and Maharajas like *Jammu and Kashmir.* Some States were under the rule of Nawabs and Nizams such as Hyderabad, Junagadh, Bhopal and others. Around 300 other Indian States were Estates or Jagirs granted by the Rulers as rewards for services to particular individuals or families. The common feature that distinguished the Princely States (also referred to as Indian States) from the Provinces of the British India was that the *Princely States had not been annexed by the British Crown.* They were allowed to remain under the personal rule of their Chiefs, Princes and Nawabs, *under the 'suzerainty' of the Crown,* as against the *provinces of British India* which were *annexed* and brought under direct British control.

'Paramountcy' was the term to describe the relationship between the Crown and the Princely States, after the assumption of suzerainty by the Crown over those States (Basu 1997: 45). The relationship was such that the *Crown accepted the responsibility for external relations and defence while the Princely States were responsible for their own internal administration.* The Crown interfered with internal administration *basically in cases of misrule and mal-administration etc;* otherwise not. On the other hand, the *Provinces in the British India were under the direct rule of the Crown* through their representatives and according to the statutes of Parliament and enactments of the Indian Legislatures.

Thus, there was hardly any similarity between the Princely States and the Provinces that constituted the rest of India. Even by the federal scheme envisaged in the Act of 1935, which was implemented partially, there was a difference. The *accession of the Princely States to the Federal scheme was voluntary,* while it was compulsory or automatic for the Provinces. Besides, the power exercised by the Federation over the Princely States was to be defined by the *Instruments of Accession,* which could even limit the authority of the Federation over the Princely States in certain areas.

It is important to note that the Act of 1935 *prescribed a federation* taking both the Provinces and the Princely States as units. Autonomy was given to the Provinces since 1937, because of which the Provinces were no longer delegates of the Central Government, but were autonomous units of administration.

But the Rulers of the *Princely States never gave their consent for their accession* to the proposed Federation.

Thus, the Federation envisaged by the Act of 1935 for both the British India Provinces and the Princely States never came true, and this part of the Act was finally abandoned when the Second World War broke out in 1939.

Cripps Mission and Cabinet Mission on Princely States

Sir Stafford Cripps, a member of the British cabinet came to India in 1942 and made it clear that the *Princely States would be left free to retain their separate status*, and that his plan would be *confined to settling the political destinies of British India only.*

But the Cabinet Mission, also referred to as Cabinet Delegation, where Sir Cripps was also a member, came to India in 1946 and recommended that there should be a Union of India, uniting both British India Provinces and the Princely States; the *Union would deal only with three subjects viz. Foreign Affairs, Defence and Communications,* while the *Princely States would retain all powers other than these.* It was the perception of the Cabinet Mission that in the changed context of World War II and new political developments in India, the Princely States would be ready to cooperate with the idea of formation of the Union of India.

Princely States start joining India

The perception of the Cabinet Mission seemed correct since most of the Princely States soon realized that it was no longer possible for them to maintain their independent existence and that it was in their interest to accede to either of the two

Dominions, India or Pakistan. As for the Princely States situated within the geographical boundaries of the Dominion of India, most of them acceded to the Dominion of India by 15 August 1947. Some Princely States who initially showed reluctance to join and were toying with the idea of remaining independent of both India and Pakistan were the Princely States of *Travancore–Cochin, Bhopal* and *Jodhpur*. However, Patel, Nehru and Patel's Secretary V.P. Menon, with the unstinted support of Lord Mountbatten, managed to work on these Princely States with love and veiled threat, as appropriate. Consequently, all three of them joined the Dominion of India before 15 August 1947.

Princely States that stayed independent on 15 August 1947

The three major Princely States that did not join either of the Dominions by 15 August 1947 were Kashmir, Hyderabad and Junagadh.

The Princely State of Hyderabad ruled by Nizam Osman Ali Khan, Asaf Jah VII did resist joining India. The leaders in the 'Dominion of Pakistan' also encouraged the Nizam to exercise the option of not joining India. Sardar Patel always knew the strategic importance of keeping Hyderabad in the Dominion of India. After all, Hyderabad was a Hindu-majority state ruled by a Muslim Nizam, and it was the biggest Princely State, geographically almost at the centre of the country. Srinath Raghavan, Senior Fellow at Centre for Policy Research, wrote in *The Print* on 26 June 2018, as follows:

'Indeed, Patel believed that Hyderabad was of greater interest than Kashmir. Until late 1947, he was open to allowing

Kashmir's accession to Pakistan if the Pakistanis would tell the Nizam of Hyderabad to fall in line and join India.' Srinath Raghavan further continued, 'Patel even stated this publicly after the occupation of Junagadh on 11 November 1947: "Our reply was that one could agree on Kashmir if they could agree on Hyderabad."'

However that did not work. Pakistan did not relent. The Nizam of Hyderabad remained indecisive. Meanwhile, Sardar Patel acted decisively and sent Major General J.N. Chaudhuri of the Indian Army to Hyderabad to take action against the Razakars, the anti-India elements in the State of Hyderabad. Major General Chaudhuri did his job dutifully and the Indian troops overcame the Razakars in a 'police action' codenamed Operation Polo between 13 and 17 September 1947. The fact that the Nizam also did not like the Razakars who were opposed to him, did help. The Nizam finally joined the Indian Dominion by signing an Instrument of Accession. Sardar Patel did not have to bargain Kashmir to get Hyderabad, and thereafter he wholeheartedly concentrated on Kashmir's accession to India.

Next was the case of Junagadh in the Kathiawar region of Gujarat, which had a Muslim Nawab, Muhammad Mahabat Khanji III, ruling over a Hindu-majority population. Junagadh was surrounded by Hindu-dominated areas on three sides, the fourth side being the coast line that included the much-revered Hindu temple of Somnath. Its port of Veeraval was just about 300 nautical miles from Karachi. The Nawab's Dewan Sir Shah Nawaz Bhutto, a leading Muslim League leader, advised the Nawab to stay out of the Indian Union. Incidentally, Sir

Shah Nawaz Bhutto was the father of Zulfikar Ali Bhutto, later Prime Minister of Pakistan. On 14 August 1947, the Nizam of Junagadh announced that his Princely State would accede to Pakistan (Guha 2008: 49). Sardar Patel got into the act. He got first some neighbouring Hindu Princely States integrated into India. The Nawab and most of his family left for Pakistan on 24 October. The Indian Army entered Junagarh on 9 November 1947; then a plebiscite was held in Junagarh on 20 February 1948. As many as 91% of the Princely State's voters voted for accession to India whereas the Hindu population was around 70%, thus indicating that a good percentage of Muslims too voted for India. The fact that a good percentage of Muslims voted for remaining with India in fact strengthened India's 'One Nation Theory'. Junagadh handed over its administration to the Indian Government in the later part of 1947.

Integration of Princely States with India

Thus, thanks to the Home Minister Sardar Patel, Prime Minister Nehru and V.P. Menon, Secretary in the Ministry of States, the process of accession of all the Princely States except Kashmir was completed. The next job of integration of the Princely States with other contiguous states was completed by following the *Patel Scheme*, formulated by Sardar Patel.

Briefly, 216 Princely States were merged into the respective provinces that were geographically contiguous to them. In the second category, 61 Princely States were converted into *Centrally Administrative Areas*. In the third category, 275 Princely States were consolidated into new viable units known as *Union of States*.

The next hurdle was to fit these Princely States into the Constitutional structure of India. In respect of the latter two groups of 336 (61 + 275) merged States, there was not much of a difficulty. In terms of an agreement between the Government of India and the Ruler of each Princely State so merged, the Rulers voluntarily agreed to the merger and *ceded all powers for the governance* of the States to the Dominion Government, reserving merely certain political rights and privileges for themselves.

However the situation was different in the case of the 216 merged Princely States. At the time of the accession to the Dominion of India in 1947, the States had acceded only on three subjects—Defence, Foreign Affairs and Communications; other subjects were to be in the domain of the States. But after the merger, the Rulers found it beneficial to have a closer connection with the Union of India. So, all the Rajpramukhs (Rulers), including the Maharaja of Mysore, signed *revised 'Instruments of Accession'*, by which all these States acceded to the Dominion of India, in *respect of all matters.*

The process of integration culminated in the *Indian Constitution Act of 1956* (seventh Amendment) whereby the Princely States lost their individual identity and became part of one uniform political organization embodied in the Indian Constitution. It may be mentioned in this context that the last vestiges of the princely order in India were done away with in December 1971, when Mrs Indira Gandhi was the Prime Minister, by abolishing the Privy Purses and certain other personal privileges accorded to the former rulers under the Constitution.

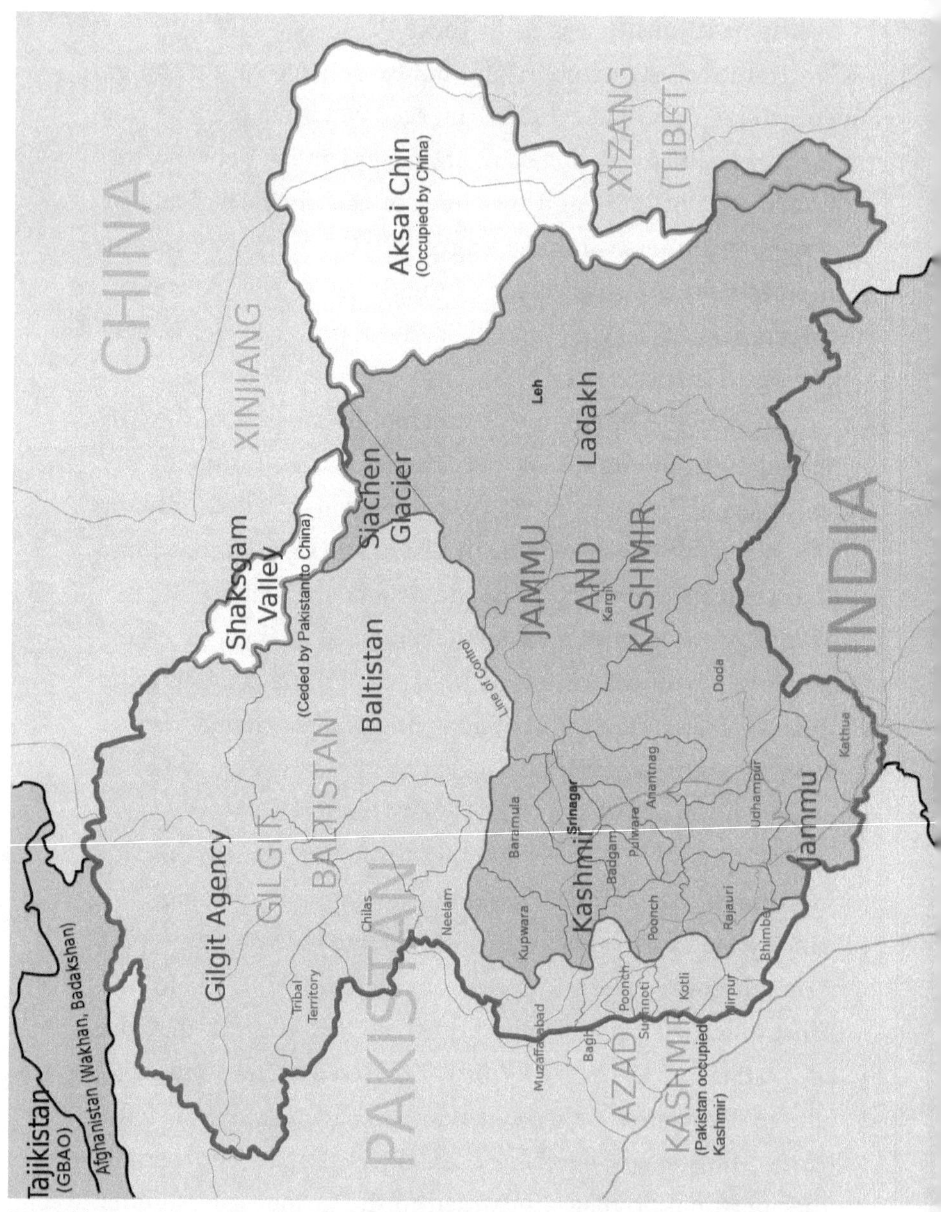

Map of the erstwhile Jammu & Kashmir state showing areas occupied by Pakistan and China

This map does not depict the International boundaries of India as defined by the Government of India. For the latest maps issued by the Government of India, see pp.14, 24.

Disclaimer: Map is for representative purposes only; map not to scale. Source: Wikimedia Commons

CHAPTER-II

The Kashmir Scenario

Geopolitical importance of Kashmir

The Princely State of Jammu & Kashmir (henceforth referred to as Kashmir at most places) has five main geographical regions with cultural and religious heterogeneity—the Valley of *Kashmir* at the centre, *Jammu* with low hills and arable land in the south, *Ladakh including Aksai Chin* with high mountains at the east, the high altitude tract of Gilgit at the north-west and another high altitude tract of *Baltistan* at the north.

A clan of Dogra Rajputs from Jammu yoked these disparate regions into a single state in the 19th century, which they gained as a result of the decline of the Sikh Empire after the death of Maharaja Ranjit Singh and the signing of the Treaty of Amritsar between the British East India Company and the Dogra ruler Raja Gulab Singh of Jammu in 1846. Thus the Princely State of Jammu & Kashmir was unified by the Dogra kings, and it became the second largest Princely State, after Hyderabad.

The Princely State of Kashmir became strategically very important for India, Pakistan, China, and even Afghanistan. These countries apart, the British and the Russians too developed an interest in Kashmir because of its geopolitical and strategic location. After 15 August 1947, the Dogra Maharaja's

Jammu & Kashmir State had borders with Pakistan to the west, Afghanistan to the north-west, the Chinese Sinkiang (Xinjiang) to the north and north-east, Tibet to the east and the rest of India to the south. Besides, the Soviet Union was separated from it by a very narrow tract of Afghanistan near the north-west tip of Gilgit. Such was the strategic location of the Dogra King's Kashmir! (Please see the map on p.32).

Political developments—rise of Sheikh Abdullah

After the Partition on 15 August 1947, some of the large Princely States, including Kashmir, started toying with the idea of remaining independent. The Princely State of Kashmir had borders with both India and Pakistan, both of whom were trying to get the accession of Kashmir to its Dominion.

On 15 August 1947 Maharaja Hari Singh was the ruler of Kashmir. He had ascended the throne of Kashmir in 1925, after the death of his uncle Maharaja Pratap Singh. His Prime Minister was Ram Chandra Kak, a Kashmiri Pandit. Hari Singh had a strong dislike for Sheikh Mohammed Abdullah, a young man from a Kashmiri village, born in 1905. Sheikh Abdullah, in spite of being well qualified with a Master's degree in Science from the Aligarh Muslim University could not get a job, like many other educated Kashmiris from the valley. A feeling of deprivation started growing among the educated Kashmiri Muslim youth. Sheikh Abdullah got drawn into a Muslim movement demanding jobs and justice from the Hindu Maharaja. With the help of some Muslim leading lights, including Sheikh Abdullah, the Jammu & Kashmir Muslim Conference was formed in 1932. Later, in

1938, Sheikh Abdullah took the lead in transforming it into a vibrant and more inclusive organization, and named it 'National Conference', which had Kashmiri Hindus and Sikhs too as members, besides Kashmiri Muslims. It was around that time that Nehru met Sheikh Abdullah and they became good friends almost instantly, mainly because of their common commitments to Hindu-Muslim harmony and socialist views.

With the increasing popularity of Sheikh Abdullah, the Maharaja's dislike for him also grew. In between, Sheikh Abdullah had been in and out of jail through the 1930s and mid-1940s. Around 1946, he asked the Dogra dynasty to quit Kashmir, and hand over power to the people. Amidst the popular unrest that grew rapidly, Maharaja declared Martial Law and Sheikh Abdullah was sentenced to three years' imprisonment. Nehru got angry and rushed to Kashmir. But he was stopped at the border and sent back by the Maharaja's men.

Maharaja's dream to remain independent

When it was clear that the British would leave by 1947, Ram Chandra Kak, the Maharaja's Prime Minister advised him to remain independent, to which the Maharaja announced in July 1946 that the Kashmiris would work out their destiny without any dictation from any quarter. This announcement disturbed the Congress leaders, including Nehru. Even the British Resident at Srinagar reported in November 1946 that the Maharaja and his Prime Minister were seriously considering the eventuality of Kashmir not joining either India or Pakistan. Thus, the Prince being Hindu did not automatically make him chose to join India just as this factor of religion initially did not provide an automatic choice in the case of Travancore-Cochin, Mysore, Jodhpur, etc.

The Maharaja was in a deep Hamletian dilemma—to join India or not. He could not join Pakistan since he thought that joining Pakistan might seal the fate of his Hindu dynasty. As for joining India, he disliked the Congress in general, and Nehru in particular for his socialist ideas, which were similar to that of Sheikh Abdullah. Thus, the Maharaja being of the same religion as the majority of the Indian population was not really working in Kashmir, much to the chagrin of fundamentalists on both sides. The good news was that Sheikh Abdullah and his party, the National Conference had secular and socialist views.

Mountbatten, having been friendly with Maharaja Hari Singh since their student days in 1921–22, set off for Kashmir in June 1947. But Mountbatten's visit was a failure. While Mountbatten sought to advise Maharaja Hari Singh to join India, Ram Chandra Kak, the Prime Minister of Kashmir told him firmly that Kashmir would like to remain independent. The Maharaja did not even meet Mountbatten on the ground of his illness (Jagmohan 1994: 82). While both Nehru and Gandhi sought to visit Kashmir to break the deadlock, only Gandhi was allowed to visit the State by Maharaja Hari Singh on the condition that he would not address any public meeting during his stay in Kashmir.

Standstill Agreement

While Jammu & Kashmir did not accede either to India or Pakistan on 15 August 1947, it offered to sign a *standstill agreement* with both India and Pakistan, which would allow free movement of people and goods across the borders. Pakistan signed the agreement. India followed a 'wait and watch' policy, and did not sign immediately.

Meanwhile, the Maharaja's relationship with Pakistan soured, he began leaning towards India and—on India's advice—he replaced his Prime Minister Ram Chandra Kak with Major General Janak Singh in August 1947 (who asked to be relieved after Pakistan-assisted raiders invaded the State). Janak Singh was replaced by Mehr Chand Mahajan, who was close to the Congress and particularly Nehru and Patel, on 15 October 1947. On 27 September 1947, Nehru informed Patel in a detailed letter about the dangerous and deteriorating situation in Kashmir; he also mentioned Pakistan's plan to send infiltrators across the border to foment trouble. Under the circumstances, Nehru wrote that the Maharaja should release Sheikh Abdullah from prison, establish a cordial relationship with him and the Maharaja should accede to India with Sheikh Abdullah's support. Sheikh Abdullah was released on 29 September. By early October, Patel wrote to Nehru that on the Kashmir issue, he and Nehru had no difference of opinion. The British Commander of the state forces of Kashmir, General Henry Scott, also reported that the National Conference was pro-Congress and anti-Pakistan.

Afridi Invasion

But the Maharaja was still in his own world with dreams of independent Kashmir. R.L. Batra, his Deputy Prime Minister, said in Delhi, on 12 October 1947, that Kashmir would not like to join either of the two countries. But if one side or the other decides to use force against them, the Maharaja may change his mind. His message was very clear. It may not be mere coincidence that around two weeks after these words were spoken, Kashmir was invaded on 22 October, by men from Pakistan across the border with the North West Frontier Province. They were a group of different Pathan tribes, collectively known as Afridis. These Afridis marched towards the south and south-east, avoiding the high mountains. Without much resistance from the Maharaja's forces, the invaders reached Muzaffarabad, now the capital of Pakistan Occupied Kashmir (POK). Soon they reached Uri and Poonch, where they got some sympathy and support from a sizeable section of the Muslim-dominated region, and as *Alastair Lamb,* the historian on Kashmir wrote, the invaders did exactly what might be expected from warriors engaged on what they saw as a 'jihad', holy war. But on reaching Baramulla, they invaded the houses of peace-loving Kashmiri Muslims as well, in addition to those of the Hindus. They looted, plundered and raped too. Thus, the tragic events at Baramulla were, in a great measure, a 'strategic and propaganda disaster for the invaders' (Guha 2008: 68).

As for the identity of the invaders, Pakistan expectedly denied any involvement, and sought to pass it on as the act of some spirited Pathans jumping to the support of their Muslim brethren who were suffering from the 'tyranny of the Hindu King'. But going by the extent of the invasion, the large number of invaders, huge quantities of arms, ammunition and other supplies carried in a large number of trucks, one cannot pass it off just as a 'juvenile attempt of a handful of Islamists'.

It's important to clarify here, even after the British Raj was over, for a certain period a sizeable strength of British Army continued in both India and Pakistan (Dogra 2015: 61–2). An invasion of this scale must have happened with prior knowledge, if not the outright instigation of Pakistan. Even the remnants of the British Army working in Pakistan, known for their efficiency, could not have been inefficient enough not to have prior information of this invasion. Be that as it may, this invasion caused a rude awakening of Maharaja Hari Singh from his dream of continuing to rule Jammu & Kashmir independently. He knew, he had to act decisively now. All resistance in his mind against acceding to either of the two countries broke down.

First, the Maharaja sent two letters, one to Prime Minister of India, Pandit Nehru and the other to Home Minister Sardar Patel seeking military help; the letters were carried by Kashmir's Deputy Prime Minister R.L. Batra. On receipt of the letters, there was an emergency meeting of India's Defence Committee, headed by the Governor General Lord Mountbatten and the members included Nehru, Patel, Defence Minister Baldev Singh and Minister without portfolio N. Gopalaswami Ayyangar. The Defence Committee sent Secretary in the Ministry of the States V.P. Menon and Major Sam Manekshaw (who later became the first Field Marshal of India) to Srinagar to make an 'on the spot study' and report back. Mehr Chand Mahajan, the Prime Minister of Kashmir apprised Menon and Manekshaw of the perilous situation and pleaded for India's help.

Menon and Manekshaw returned on 25 October 1947 and suggested sending troops. On 26 October, Mahajan flew into

Delhi and there was a breakfast meeting with Nehru, Patel and Menon. Mahajan pleaded for military help and also proposed immediate accession of Kashmir to India. The Defence Committee met later in the morning of 26 October, and decided that Indian army troops would be flown to Srinagar the next morning, 27 October 1947. The States Ministry was directed to prepare an Instrument of Accession for the Maharaja to sign and a letter emphasizing that Kashmir's accession would be temporary, pending ascertainment of the 'will of the people' of Kashmir.

Shortly after the meeting of the Defence Committee on the morning of 26 October 1947, Menon and Mahajan flew to Jammu, where the Maharaja had shifted from Srinagar the previous night. The Maharaja was ready to accede at once, and handed over his letter to the Governor General (Lord Mountbatten) requesting for accession and also duly signed the Instrument of Accession. With these documents, Menon flew back to Delhi the same day. Patel who was waiting at the airport took Menon straight to a meeting of the Defence Committee that was arranged for the evening of the same day i.e. 26 October 1947. The decision to send troops to Srinagar was confirmed. It was also separately decided to accept the Instrument of Accession.

The Maharaja joins India

As mentioned, on 26 October 1947, Maharaja Hari Singh wrote to Lord Mountbatten, the Governor General of India seeking help and support of the Indian Dominion (Noorani 2014: 41–3). Obviously the help he had sought was in terms of men, material and military equipment. He also sought to get the Princely State of Jammu & Kashmir acceded to the Indian Union since he was aware that without such accession, India could not have helped him. He even attached the Instrument of Accession for acceptance of the Indian Government.

The relevant extracts of this important letter are reproduced below.

> I have to inform your Excellency that a grave emergency has arisen in my State and request immediate assistance of your Government.
>
> The mass infiltration of tribesmen drawn from the distant areas of the N.W.F. Province coming regularly in Motor Trucks using Mansehra-Muzaffarabad road and fully armed with up-to-date weapons cannot possibly be done without the knowledge of the Provincial Government of the N.W.F. Province and the Government of Pakistan. In spite of repeated appeals made by my Government no attempt has been made to check these raiders or stop them from coming to my State. In fact both the Pakistan Radio and Press have reported these occurrences. The Pakistan Radio even put out a story that a Provisional Government has been set up in Kashmir. The people of my State, both the Muslims and non-Muslims, generally have taken no part at all.
>
> With the conditions obtaining at present in my State and the great emergency of the situation as it exists, I have no option but to ask for help from the

> Indian Dominion. Naturally they cannot send the help asked for by me without my State acceding to the Dominion of India. I have accordingly decided to do so and I attach the Instrument of Accession for acceptance by your government.

The Maharaja's intention of engaging Sheikh Abdullah in the future functioning of the State government after accession to India was also expressed in the following near-concluding lines in the letter.

> I may also inform your Excellency's Government that it is my intention at once to set up an Interim Government and ask Sheikh Abdullah to carry the responsibilities in this emergency with my Prime Minister.
>
> If my State has to be saved, immediate assistance must be available at Srinagar.
>
> (Noorani 2014: 41–3)

The concluding sentence was significant: '*In haste and with kind regards. Hari Singh*'. The Maharaja was indeed in haste, after a delay of so many months.

After consulting Nehru, Patel and others concerned, Lord Mountbatten replied on 27 October 1947, accepting the accession of Kashmir State to the Dominion of India. He also pointed out that as soon as law and order is restored in Kashmir and the invaders are driven out, the question of accession should be settled by reference to the people. The relevant extract of his letter is reproduced below.

In the special circumstances mentioned by your Highness, my Government have decided to accept the accession of Kashmir State to the Dominion of India. Consistently with their policy that, in the case of any State where the issue of accession has been the subject of dispute, the question of accession should be decided in accordance with the wishes of the people of the State, it is my Government's wish that, as soon as law and order have been restored in Kashmir and her soil cleared of the invader, the question of the State's accession should be settled by a reference to the people. Meanwhile, in response to Your Highness's appeal for military aid, action has been taken today to send troops of the Indian Army to Kashmir to help your own forces to defend your territory and to protect the lives, property and honour of your people.

(Noorani 2014: 43)

The Governor General also expressed his satisfaction about inviting Sheikh Abdullah to form an Interim Government in the last para of his letter: '*My Government and I note with satisfaction that your Highness has decided to invite Sheikh Abdullah to form an Interim Government to work with your Prime Minister.*' (Noorani: 2014: 43)

Circumstances that helped the Maharaja

Before going to the third important document i.e. the Instrument of Accession of Kashmir, let us recollect the circumstances and critical documents that helped the Maharaja to retain some elements of sovereignty. As explained in the Prologue, during the British Rule from 1858, there were basically two parts—British India comprising Provinces and a few Tribal Areas directly under the British Crown, and secondly, some 565 Princely States of different categories. The British Crown had suzerainty over these 565 states, broadly to the effect that the Crown controlled three departments of Defence, Foreign Affairs and Communications, and the remaining departments including internal administrative matters were controlled by the Princely States. These Princely States together constituted about a third of the entire British Indian Empire. When the British decided to leave India, it was made clear by the British Cabinet Mission in May 1946 that with the departure of the British, the Princely States would become, to all intents and purposes, independent, and that they would have the option to refuse to accede to any of the regimes that takes over from the British.

Further, the Government of India Act, 1935, had dealt with in good detail the process of integration of the Princely States into the Indian Dominion (at that time, there was no talk of a separate 'Pakistan Dominion') through a federal structure. In this context, it may be recalled that in pursuance of the Indian Independence Act of 1947, the Government of India Act of 1935 was made applicable, through Adaptation Orders, for the period of time taken in framing the Constitution by the Constituent Assembly. So, the provisions of the Act of 1935 relating to the Princely States got its new lease of life by these Adaptation Orders.

Further, the *Government of India Act, 1935,* as adapted on 15 August, 1947 by the *India Order (Provisional Constitution),*

1947 lucidly explains certain matters relating to the Instrument of Accession in general for all the Princely States. The extract of *Sections 6 (2) and 6 (3)* of the said Act is reproduced below:

> 6. Accession of Indian States:-
>
> (2) An Instrument of Accession shall specify the matters which the Ruler accepts as matters with respect to which the Dominion Legislature may make laws for the State, and the limitations, if any, to which the power of the Dominion Legislature to make laws for the State, and the exercise of the executive authority of the Dominion in the State, are respectively to be subject.
>
> (3) *A Ruler may, by a supplementary Instrument executed by him and accepted by the Governor-General vary the Instrument of Accession of his State by extending the functions which by virtue of that Instrument are exercisable by any Dominion authority in relation to his State.*

In brief, the Sections 6 (2) and 6 (3) mean that the Instrument of Accession will specify the areas/subjects where the Dominion Legislature (read Centre) will create legislation and the areas where the State Legislature (read Princely State) will make the law. Further, the ruler may under certain conditions vary the Instrument of Accession subsequently.

Maharaja Hari Singh in his letter dated *26 October* addressed to the Governor General, had attached the Instrument of Accession. *He took care to make the Instrument of Accession different from those in respect of other Princely*

States. The *clauses 7 and 8* of the Instrument which show this clearly, are quoted below.

> *7. Nothing in this Instrument shall be deemed to commit me in any way to acceptance of any future constitution of India or to fetter my discretion to enter into arrangements with the Government of India under any such future constitution.*
>
> *8. Nothing in this Instrument affects the continuance of my sovereignty in and over this State, or, save as provided by or under this Instrument, the exercise of any powers, authority and rights now enjoyed by me as Ruler of this State or the validity of any law at present in force in this State.*
>
> (Noorani 2014: 38–9)

Further, through Clause 3 of the said Instrument, the Maharaja accepted that on matters specified in the Schedule annexed to the Instrument, the Dominion Legislature of India may make laws for the State. The matters were Defence, External Affairs, Communications and certain Ancillary matters. Another noteworthy matter is that the Maharaja has used the expression 'Sovereignty' at two places in the Instrument of Accession.

In the beginning of the third para, he announced as follows:

'Now Therefore I Ruler of _____ *in the exercise of my sovereignty in and over my said State* Do hereby execute this my Instrument of Accession, and ...' *(emphasis added)*.

Again in Clause 8, the Maharaja said, 'Nothing in this Instrument *affects the continuance of my sovereignty* in and over this State...' *(emphasis added)* (Noorani 2014: 37–9).

The documents discussed ahead are the following:

1. Maharaja's letter dated 26.10.1947 to the Governor General for acceptance of his request for accession to India.
2. The Governor General Lord Mountbatten's reply dated 27.10.1947 accepting the Maharaja's request;
3. Guidelines on framing the Instrument of Accession by the Princely States as given at Sections 6 (2) & (3) of the Government of India Act, 1935, as adapted, and
4. The Instrument of Accession of the State of Jammu & Kashmir signed on 26.10.1947 by the Maharaja.

(Noorani 2014: 37–41)

Four Documents that had a strong bearing on introducing Article 370

A careful study of these four documents will reveal that *all these four documents and the events revolving around these documents have a strong bearing on the introduction of Article 370 in the Indian Constitution.* Mention may be made of two important features at this stage.

In terms of the Instrument of Accession, the Maharaja retained sovereignty over the State of Jammu & Kashmir, although the use of the term 'sovereignty' did cause a controversy. It is important to note that Kashmir had its own Constitution, even when it was under the suzerainty of the British Crown. On 7 September 1939 Maharaja Hari Singh had promulgated a royal constitution because of certain political developments including people's unrest. The Jammu & Kashmir Constitution Act, 1939, was rather elaborate, and it was clearly a king's constitution.

A Separate Constitution

After the British left, it was expected that this Act of 1939 would also lapse, along with the Constitution of Kashmir. But, interestingly, both the Maharaja and Sheikh Abdullah agreed that by the terms of accession, Kashmir had a right to its own Constitution; the only critical difference in their views was that the Maharaja wanted to continue with the old constitution while Sheikh Abdullah preferred a new modern constitution with modern ideas to be framed by a new Constituent Assembly. No doubt, like other Princely States, Kashmir had also sent its representatives to the country's Constituent Assembly in June 1949. But, that Kashmir was on a different footing was made clear by its representatives, when they said that their association with India would be based only in terms of Clause 7 of the Instrument of Accession.

Requirement of Plebiscite

Another exceptional feature associated with Kashmir's accession to India was the requirement of having a plebiscite soon after the normalcy returns in the State. This condition was not there in the Instrument of Accession signed by the Maharaja. But it was expressly present in the letter dated 27 October 1947 from Lord Mountbatten, the Governor General addressed to the Maharaja.

The term 'reference to the people' used in the letter from Mountbatten basically meant 'plebiscite'. It may be recalled, there was already a precedent; plebiscite had already been conducted in the case of accession of the Princely State of Junagadh, where the people had voted conclusively in favour of joining India. Junagadh was a princely state where the ruler (Nawab) was a Muslim and among the subjects, the Hindus were in majority. So, it was felt incumbent upon the Indian political leaders to have a plebiscite for Kashmir as well; Kashmir was a state where the ruler (Maharaja) was a Hindu and among the subjects, the Muslims were in a majority. It may be mentioned in this context that some people had argued that the purpose of plebiscite was served subsequently in the Assembly elections in Kashmir held in 1951, 1957, 1962, etc., where the National Conference and parties which were pro-India had continuously won the Assembly elections handsomely.

The Governor General had stated that the policy of the Government of India has been to get the question of accession decided 'in accordance with the wishes of the people of the State' in a case where the issue of accession has been a subject of dispute. The Governor General further stated that it was his Government's wish that the question of the State's accession should be settled by a reference to the people. The expressions 'by a reference to the people' and 'in accordance with the wishes of the people' indicate the plebiscite to be a promise by the Governor General for accession. It further appears that the Indian leaders saw a strong possibility of Sheikh Abdullah's National Conference winning the plebiscite because of its popularity among the masses. By that time, it was clear that the National Conference was in favour of Kashmir joining India, and not Pakistan. That is why the Indian leaders thought of closing the chapter on controversy forever by the plebiscite, and thereby have the accession of the entire State of Jammu & Kashmir confirmed. Further, a Muslim-majority border state voting for accession to India would be in line with India's commitment to the 'one-nation theory' as against Pakistan's 'two-nation theory'. Another aim was to strengthen the Indian military domination in the entire state, including the international border areas like Gilgit-Baltistan and 'Azad Kashmir'. After all, the fact of accession conferred a legal right for the Indian troops to enter and operate in the entire State of Jammu & Kashmir.

As mentioned before, for quite a few months even after independence on 15 August, the armies of both India and Pakistan continued to have British Commanders-in-Chief. *Sir Claude Auchinleck* was chief of the united military supreme command for both the Indian Army and Pakistan Army. *Sir Douglas Gracey* was the Commander-in-Chief of the Pakistan Army (Lamb 1992: 141).

After Kashmir's accession, when the Indian Army took charge in Kashmir, and the Afridi invasion was going on, Mohammed Ali Jinnah, the Governor General of Pakistan ordered General Gracey to send troops to Kashmir. But General Gracey was advised by the Army Supreme Commander Auchinleck to tell Jinnah that if Pakistan regulars went to Kashmir, all British army officers would have to resign from the Pakistan Army. Upon hearing this Jinnah relented.

Meanwhile, in early October 1947, the Maharaja complained to Pakistan's Foreign Ministry about the infiltration by the Afridis inside the border in the Jammu region. Pakistan denied the allegation and called the Maharaja's attention to 'terror and atrocities perpetuated by J&K forces against the Muslim population of Poonch'.

A new leader emerged in Sardar Ibrahim Khan, a member of the J&K Legislature, as the head of the 'Poonch Liberation Movement'. He united the different factions in Poonch and maintained contact with the Pakistan Muslim League. He was instrumental in establishing an 'Azad Kashmir' government in Rawalpindi.

As relations with Kashmir worsened, Pakistan suspected that the Maharaja would accede to India. Added to that, in light of Sheikh Abdullah's animosity towards the Muslim League and Pakistan, and his avowed choice of joining the secular and socialistic dominion of India, Pakistan decided to seize Kashmir by force. Thus happened the Afridi invasion and the start of the first war between India and Pakistan over Kashmir.

The Afridi invasion backed by the Pakistani Army was successfully repulsed by the Indian Army led by Lt. Col. Dewan Ranjit Rai. The volunteers of the Abdullah-led National Conference aided the Indian Army with specific information to drive out the invaders.

In a surprise move, General Gracey, Commander-in-Chief of the Pakistan Army, who had defied Jinnah's order in October 1947, advised the Pakistan government on 20 April 1948 to move its forces into J&K, since his information was that India was about to launch a general offensive against Pakistan in Kashmir. Pakistan did move forces and thus the full-fledged war began. However, the National Conference and its leader Sheikh Abdullah, who had become Prime Minister of Kashmir in March 1948, continuously held the view that Kashmir should remain united with India with maximum possible autonomy. Mehr Chand Mahajan had written in his book *Looking Back*, that Abdullah was completely against the idea of merging the state with Pakistan since the then largely secular Kashmiri populace did not buy Jinnah's 'two-nation theory'.

In these circumstances, Mountbatten went to Lahore, on 1 November 1947, to meet Jinnah and Liaquat Ali Khan, the Prime Minister of Pakistan, to discuss the Kashmir crisis. Both Nehru and Patel decided to avoid going over to Lahore, for different reasons. In the meeting of the two Governors General, Mountbatten *suggested to Jinnah that the Kashmir issue be settled by a plebiscite under the supervision of the United Nations,* after the restoration of normalcy.

This obviously meant withdrawal of the Afridi invaders from Kashmir and also Pakistan's stopping their help to the aggressors. Jinnah developed cold feet, most probably because the Pakistani leaders had a mistrust of Sheikh Abdullah. They were aware of his capability to 'manipulate the plebiscite' in favour of India with the full support of his party National Conference, which was secular in character and likely to vote for accession to India.

Nehru had followed up the endeavours of Lord Mountbatten by indicating to Liaquat Ali Khan, the Prime Minister of Pakistan, in early December 1947 that he was seriously considering the invitation of UN observers to come to India and advise on the proposed plebiscite. Liaquat Ali Khan knew that the plebiscite would most likely be in favour of India, thanks to the efforts of Nehru and Sheikh Abdullah. So, he did not show much interest in this idea.

UN Intervention sought

By the end of December 1947 Nehru moved the United Nations complaining against the Pakistani aggression in Kashmir, and sought UN mediation in the Kashmir dispute; advice on conducting a plebiscite was also sought. In January, 1948, there was the first UN Resolution which merely asked both India and Pakistan to sort out their differences and not to aggravate the situation. The subsequent UN Resolution of February 1948 did not help much. Then there was the *UN Commission for India and Pakistan (UNCIP)* Plan of August 1948.

Throughout 1948, the war in Kashmir continued; even Pakistan publicly admitted its involvement in July 1948. Finally, on 1 January 1949, Nehru agreed to a ceasefire. The terms of the ceasefire, laid out in a UN Commission Resolution on 13 August 1948 were adopted by the Commission on 5 January 1949. It was a three-part resolution, amending the UN Security Council Resolution 47. The steps were to be as follows:

- In the first step, Pakistan was asked to withdraw all its nationals that entered Kashmir for the sake of fighting.
- In the second step, India was asked to progressively reduce its forces to the minimum level required for law and order.
- In the third step, India was asked to appoint a Plebiscite Administrator nominated by the United Nations who would conduct a free and impartial plebiscite.

The first step in terms of the aforementioned UN Resolution on Ceasefire was never taken by Pakistan. In this context, some critics have pointed out that Prime Minister Nehru had the legal authority to exercise the legality of the Instrument of Accession vis-a-vis the whole of Jammu and Kashmir including the parts which were under the administration of Pakistan like POK, Gilgit, Baltistan etc. So, he could have gone ahead with annexation of the aforesaid areas when the invaders were being driven out, instead of declaring a ceasefire. This criticism became valid particularly when Pakistan did not even comply with the first step of vacating the occupied territories of Kashmir. The critics wonder why Nehru did not continue the counter-attack and push the border back to the original border of Jammu & Kashmir as it was when Maharaja Hari Singh acceded to India on 27 October 1947. They also question why Nehru chose to take the issue to UN arbitration. The defendants of Nehru's action however claim that Nehru hoped that the international community would recognize Pakistan's aggression and intervene to stop further bloodshed. He also hoped that a Plebiscite under UN supervision, which Nehru was sure to win with help of Sheikh Abdullah and his National Conference, would settle the Kashmir issue for good.

By the end of the war, India gained control of about two-thirds of the erstwhile Princely State of J&K, and Pakistan the remaining one-third including POK, Gilgit and Baltistan.

Towards the end of July 1948, the Indian and Pakistani military representatives signed an agreement at Karachi, defining a ceasefire line in the State of Jammu & Kashmir. The Commanders of the armies of both the countries were still British—General Bucher for India and General Gracey for Pakistan.

Soon after the ceasefire in early January, 1949 the UNCIP finalized a proposal for conducting a plebiscite under the control of a new independent body called Plebiscite Administration, headed by a Plebiscite Administrator. It was welcomed by Pakistan. But, based on the feedback about the past activities of the official chosen as Plebiscite Administrator, India had strong reservations against the chosen person, US Fleet Admiral Chester W. Nimitz, and hence rejected the proposal. Thus, the proposed plebiscite never took place.

Some facts about the Northern Frontier

Let us review the other lesser-known parts of the State of Jammu & Kashmir i.e. the *'Northern Frontier'* comprising Gilgit-Baltistan and Ladakh. It may be recalled, while presenting his proposal of abrogating Article 370 in Parliament, Amit Shah, the Home Minister had also said, inter alia, that Kashmir means the entire territory of Jammu & Kashmir and it includes Pakistan Occupied Kashmir, Gilgit and Aksai Chin.

The Northern Frontier had two routes across it—to the west ran the Giligit-Baltistan Route, and to the east and south-east ran the Ladakh Route. The whole area has always been the most strategic one, with the following countries/areas bordering it.

First, those countries/areas bordering Gilgit. It has a narrow tract of Afghanistan at the north-west tip. Beyond that narrow tract is what was known as USSR (commonly referred to as Russia). Right to the north, beyond the Karakoram Range, lay Sinkiang (Xinjiang) Province of China. The North West Frontier Provinces (NWFP) of present-day Pakistan are to the West and present-day Pakistan Occupied Kashmir is to its south-west. Kashmir Valley is to its south and Baltistan is to its east. In the north, the main populated areas are Gilgit and Hunza.

Baltistan, whose main city is Skardu, has Sinkiang (Xinjiang) Province of China in the North, Siachen Glacier and thereafter Aksai Chin (now occupied by China) of Ladakh are to the East, both Kargil and Leh of Ladakh are in the south and south-east. Part of Kashmir valley is to the south of Baltistan beyond the Zoji-La Pass, most critical from a strategic point of view.

The Kargil sector of Ladakh has Baltistan to its north and Kashmir Valley in the south. Leh sector that includes Aksai Chin in the north-east has Tibet to the east, Kashmir Valley and Jammu to the west and the rest of India to the south.

The religion of the people in different areas in Kashmir can be summed up as follows:

Leh in Ladakh is a Buddhist majority area whereas Kargil is predominantly Muslim. The Kashmir Valley has a predominantly Muslim population with Sunnis, Shiyas and Ahmediyas. In the Jammu region there are about 65% Hindus and the rest are Muslims.

Political and Military Developments

The British never annexed Kashmir; however because of its strategic location, they had *posted a British Agent*, first in Ladakh and then in Gilgit by 1877. The Gilgit Agency was put in place for Gilgit-Baltistan to supervise the conduct of policy in the Northern Frontier. In 1881, the British Agency was withdrawn because of discomfort of the Maharaja of Kashmir and other strategic reasons. Thus, the Maharaja had complete responsibility to guard the Northern Frontier from 1881. But this was short-lived. In 1889 the state was placed under the control of *a Council of State* closely supervised by a British

Resident in Srinagar. The Resident was later replaced by an Officer on Special Duty.

The Northern Frontier remained volatile and involved in war at Hunza and Sinkiang (Xinjiang) during the intervening period of 1889 to the late 1930s. Meanwhile, in 1925, Hari Singh, nephew of Maharaja Pratap Singh ascended the throne of Kashmir on his uncle's death. The relationship between the British Agent in Gilgit and the Maharaja started deteriorating fast. The dyarchy i.e. dual administration that existed then was like this—the British were concerned with defence, foreign relations and communications, while the running of the civil government through a Governor was the responsibility of the Maharaja.

Gilgit Region leased out to the British

In order to bring an end to the unpleasant relationship, finally in March 1935, the Gilgit-Baltistan region, north of the Indus was *leased out to the British for a period of 60 years*. It was *not ceded out of Maharaja's Kashmir*, but only leased out to British India. All the civil and military administration of the area was transferred to the Government of British India. It was however made clear that the leased area remained very much a part of the Maharaja's Princely State of Jammu & Kashmir; the Maharaja continued to receive certain public honours from the leased territory.

It is necessary to know about the Gilgit Agency slightly in more detail, since it had a very active role in the first week of November 1947 in deciding the fate of the Gilgit-Baltistan area. It may be recalled that the Gilgit Agency had been functioning almost continuously since 1877, either with a British Agent or a Council of State under a British Resident or an Officer on Special Duty. It had been growing in strength with each passing year (Lamb 1992: 30).

Gilgit Agency joins Pakistan

Originally, the troops under the command of the Gilgit Agency were recruited almost entirely by the State of Jammu & Kashmir. But gradually the Gilgit Agency felt the need to have its own troops. The reasons unfolded after the events in the first week of November 1947. In 1913 the Corps of Gilgit Scouts was founded by recruiting the local people of the Gilgit Agency areas. Over a period of time it became evident that Gilgit Agency was quietly creating a power centre independent of both the Maharaja's government and to a great extent, even of the Government of British India. The result was that after the independence of India on 15 August, when Maharaja Hari Singh was still undecided about accession to India, the Gilgit Agency under the leadership of Major William Brown was preparing for a sinister plan. Within a few days of Kashmir's accession to India on 27 October 1947, Major Brown in a bloodless coup d'état overthrew the Maharaja's Governor Ghansara Singh and opted for the Gilgit Agency areas joining Pakistan on 3 November 1947 and the Agency Scouts marched with him to join Pakistan. The Pakistani Political Agent, Khan Mohammed Alam Khan, came over to Gilgit on 16 November 1947 and took over the administration of Gilgit.

This was an illegal act. When Maharaja Hari Singh signed the Instrument of Accession of Kashmir to India, *the accession was for the entire State of Kashmir including Gilgit, Baltistan,* etc. He was the Sovereign King of entire Kashmir. So, Major Brown's independent decision of merging Gilgit Agency, which by then had become Indian territory, after the accession on 27 October 1947, was a blatantly illegal act.

Gilgit Scouts capture Baltistan and Kargil

The Gilgit Scouts together with the 'irregulars' from POK moved towards Baltistan and Ladakh. By May 1948, they captured Skardu, Dras and Kargil. The Indian forces which were fighting with full force in Poonch sector in the South West, liberated Poonch. Thereafter, a large Indian force was rushed to Kargil; they mounted a big offensive in the autumn of 1948, and recaptured Dras and Kargil. But Gilgit and Baltistan remained under the control of Pakistan. Two parts of the territory i.e. Gilgit and Baltistan were merged by Pakistan into a single administrative unit under the name *'Northern Areas'*.

Pakistan cedes Shaksgam Valley to China

Another significant event was in 1963, when Pakistan ceded the Shaksgam Valley tract near Hunza Area in Gilgit Agency to China, following the signing of the Sino-Pakistan Frontier Agreement. This paved the way for China to build the Karakoram Highway, which linked Kashgar, the second-most important city in China's Sinkiang (Xinjiang) province with Hasan Abdel (located a few kilometres beyond Islamabad in Pakistan). Thus, with the construction of the Karakoram Highway by China, Pakistan and China got closely connected. This was another illegal act inasmuch as Pakistan had no legal right to give away part of an illegally occupied Indian territory of Gilgit-Baltisan to a third party i.e. China.

China occupies Aksai Chin and builds a road across it

Aksai Chin is located at the north-east top corner of J&K, an area hitherto under the control of Ladakh Division of Jammu & Kashmir. The British had a particular interest in Aksai Chin, a barren land and desolate area, because of its strategic location in terms of both geographical and commercial importance. Aksai Chin provided the potential approach to entire Central Asia through Sinkiang (Xinjiang) province of China in the North and Tibet in the east. During the post-Independence years, India was thoroughly engaged in fighting with the invaders supported by Pakistan at Poonch–Uri Sector and later in Gilgit-Baltistan areas. Perhaps, that was the reason why the leaders gave less attention to the north-east tip of Ladakh—Aksai Chin. Too much trust on China and its friendship led India to believe that the Chinese won't harm India. This also resulted in gross neglect on the Aksai Chin front. The grand betrayal of the British Major in asking Pakistan to take over the Gilgit Agency and later Baltistan had also stunned India. Taking advantage of this lack of attention by India in Aksai Chin, China started constructing a highway in Aksai Chin in the early 1950s, from Tibet end in the east to the Sinkiang (Xinjiang) end in the north, and claimed the whole of Aksai Chin as a part of Chinese territory. The road was completed by 1954.

There is a background to this. During the British rule in India, the British had a major strategic interest in the northern and north-eastern border of Kashmir. The borders in these areas were undefined at many places, particularly where there was no habitation. In 1898, the Government of India started an exercise in border alignment in these areas, including Aksai Chin. Finally, in March 1899, a Note on the drawing of border line was prepared and sent by the British Minister to the Chinese Government. Henceforth, the border talks between the British and Chinese Governments proceeded on that basis. After certain refinements by 1914, the British India decided to go by that Note of 1899, as refined. Aksai Chin of Ladakh, along with the Gilgit Region, Baltistan, Kargil and Leh were always parts of the territory of the Maharaja of the Princely State of Kashmir, which automatically became part of the Indian territory since Kashmir's accession in October, 1947.

In 1954, independent India for the first time came out with a map showing Aksai Chin on the Indian side, at the north-eastern tip of Ladakh, based on certain interpretations of the *1899 Note* which was refined by Lord Curzon in 1905, and again in 1914. Based on this new map, a cartographical evidence, *Nehru wrote a letter in September, 1959 to Zhou Enlai, the Chinese Prime Minister, claiming that the whole of Aksai Chin lay in the Indian Territory* (Lamb 1992: 72). China did not pay any heed to this protest.

That the Chinese had occupied Aksai Chin and built a road across it came to be officially known much later, when an Indian Ambassador in China brought to the notice of the Government of India a publication of a small-scale map in a Chinese magazine; the map clearly showed that Aksai Chin was part of China and that a road ran through Aksai Chin from Tibet region to Sinkiang (Xinjiang) Province.

As of now, Aksai Chin continues to be part of China, while India continues to claim it to be part of the unified Princely State of Jammu & Kashmir that was acceded to India in 1947.

In the Parliamentary speech of the Home Minister on 5 August, 2019, he has categorically said in the context of abrogation of Article 370 that the State of Jammu & Kashmir includes Pakistan Occupied Kashmir areas of Gilgit-Baltistan, Muzaffarabad areas and Aksai Chin in the north-east tip of Ladakh, presently under China's occupation.

China joins Pakistan in protesting to the UN

The reason for China getting provoked by India's latest action of abrogating Article 370 lies in the two issues of Chinese occupation of Shaksgam Valley in Gilgit-Baltistan and Aksai Chin in Ladakh. China felt threatened particularly because of the Home Minister's assertion that the word Kashmir means the whole of Jammu & Kashmir, including Pakistan Occupied Kashmir (POK) and Aksai Chin.

UN Closed Consultation of August 2019

Therefore, China reacted sharply to India's action along with Pakistan. It was only Pakistan and China who took up the matter with the UN Security Council, seeking a meeting of the UNSC to discuss the developments in Kashmir.

However, the UNSC had only a 'closed consultation' meeting on the Kashmir issue, as reported in *The Hindu* dated 16 August 2019. The report was titled 'UN Security Council meeting on Kashmir. Stop terror to start talks, India tells Pakistan'.

Indian Ambassador to the UN, Syed Akbaruddin accused Pakistan and China of attempting to impart greater significance to the 'closed consultation' meeting than was warranted. On briefing the media after the Chinese and Pakistani counterparts spoke, he stated, 'After the end of the Security Council's closed consultations, we noted that two states who made national statements tried to pass them off as the will of the international community' (*The Hindu*, 16 Aug 2019).

China seems to have been peeved as it appears from the statement of China's UN envoy Zhang Jun, 'What should be pointed out is that India's action has also challenged China's sovereign interests and violated bilateral agreements,' Mr Zhang Jun said, stating China was seriously concerned about the issue (*The Hindu*, 16 Aug 2019).

Events of the past two centuries—impact on Article 370

The preceding events spanning over almost two centuries, narrated very briefly, would give the readers a fairly good idea about what was happening in India in respect of Kashmir during the British days of Princely States, and immediately after Independence. This will also help in understanding the circumstances for introducing an article like Article 370 in our Constitution. Further, one factor that has always remained our leaders' resolve, irrespective of their political affiliations, is that the entire territory of Jammu & Kashmir that was being ruled by the last ruler of Kashmir, Maharaja Hari Singh, a territory that was acceded to India in October 1947, must be with India—as it is depicted in our national map i.e., including Pakistan Occupied Kashmir, Gilgit, Baltistan and Aksai Chin.

CHAPTER- III
Birth of Articles 370 and 35A

Battle of nerves between Indian leaders and the Maharaja
The Indian political leaders, led by Nehru and Patel, rightly decided to leave no stone unturned to ensure the accession of Kashmir to India. So, the cajoling of the Maharaja started. *Ram Chandra Kak*, the Prime Minister of Kashmir, who was aiding the Maharaja in having his dreams of a free Kashmir independent of both India and Pakistan, was replaced by *Mehr Chand Mahajan* who was close to both Nehru and Patel. Finally, the proverbial 'last straw on the camel's back' was the Afridi invasion in Muzzaffarbad-Poonch of Kashmir and its initial impact with the support of Pakistan, when the Maharaja decided to seek help from India and agreed to sign an Instrument of Accession. Yet, the Maharaja had his royal spirit still high in him. Therefore, we find that even while sending his request for help in terms of men and materiel, and also for getting Kashmir acceded to India under exceptional circumstances of invasion in his territory, he had *sought to retain 'sovereignty' over his state even after ceding Kashmir to India. He has also sought to retain certain rights at Clauses 7 and 8 of the Instrument of Accession* sent to Lord Mountbatten, the Governor General of India.

Insertion of Article 370

In the foregoing circumstances, our leaders had to think of inserting an Article in our Constitution covering the promises made in the Instrument of Accession. Thus, it is unfair to question the wisdom of inserting an article, such as as Article 370 in the Constitution. *Of course, it's a different issue as to whether successive Governments at the Centre represented by almost all the major political parties including BJP, Congress, Left Parties, Janata Dal, etc., at different times should have considered it correct to continue with Article 370 in our Constitution.* However, some governments, even those led by Congress, have been diluting the provisions of Article 370 to a big extent, by making so many subjects and Articles of the Indian Constitution applicable to the State of Jammu & Kashmir.

The other point as to *whether or not* certain provisions relating to special status in *Article 370 have been correctly abrogated now on 5 and 6 August 2019,* is a separate question.

Is Article 257 of the Pakistani Constitution similar to Article 370 of the Indian Constitution?

Before proceeding further on Article 370 of the Indian Constitution, it would be interesting to have a look at *Article 257* of the Pakistani Constitution, through which special status was guaranteed for the people of the State of Jammu & Kashmir *'when the people of the State of J&K decide to accede to Pakistan'.*

In an article titled 'Jammu *& Kashmir–Paradise lost'* written on the *Website https://braintoast.wordpress.com* (dated 31 Oct 2019) a brief narrative has been given on *Article 257* of the Pakistani Constitution. Pakistan always nursed the idea that

Kashmir being a Muslim-majority Princely State would finally accede to Pakistan. Therefore, a special status was guaranteed for the people of the State of J&K, by introducing *Article 257* in the Pakistani Constitution. *Article 257* defines how the relation of the State of J&K and Pakistan would be determined: '*When the people of the State of J&K decide to accede to Pakistan, the relationship between Pakistan and the State shall be determined in accordance with the wishes of the people of that State.*'

Pakistan Administered Kashmir consists of two regions, namely Gilgit-Baltistan, formerly known as Federally Administered Northern Areas (FANA) and Azad Jammu & Kashmir, formerly known as Azad Kashmir, the western areas of Jammu & Kashmir occupied by Pakistan after the Afridi invasion of October 1947, which in India is called Pakistan Occupied Kashmir or POK.

Gilgit-Baltistan is governed by the Gilgit-Baltistan (Empowerment and Self Governance) Order, 2009, which was issued by the President of Pakistan after informal consultation with local leaders. However, Azad J&K (AJK) is being governed under the Interim Constitution Act of Azad Jammu & Kashmir Act, 1974, which was passed by the Legislative Assembly of Azad J&K, and approved by the Government of Pakistan.

Although the Pakistani Constitution claims that both these regions are autonomous, effectively the real power of Gilgit-Baltistan is controlled by a council based in Islamabad with the Prime Minister of Pakistan as its Chairman. Similarly Azad Jammu & Kashmir is vested in the Kashmir Council based in Islamabad, of which the Prime Minister of Pakistan is the head. So, these two regions cannot be said to be autonomous.

Another interesting fact is that the Maharaja of J&K had granted some special benefits to the indigenous people, one of which was through the State Subject Rule. This rule allowed only the natives of J&K, also referred to as State Subjects, to acquire permanent residence in the state. In terms of this rule, the natural resources of the State were the property of indigenous people who only had the right to utilize them without any outside reference. Pakistan abrogated the State Subject Rule in areas of Kashmir administered by them. This is how it happened.

The Gilgit-Baltistan region of the erstwhile Princely State of J&K became the northernmost administrative territory of Pakistan after the First Kashmir War of 1948; this became a separate administrative unit in 1970, known as Federally Administered Northern Areas. In 1974, the Government of Pakistan under the leadership of President Zulfiqar Ali Bhutto abrogated the State Subject Rule in Gilgit-Baltistan. This resulted in demographic changes in the territory.

In 2009, the FANA was granted limited autonomy and was renamed as Gilgit-Baltistan through the Self Governance Order signed by Pakistani President Asif Ali Zardari, son-in-law of Z.A. Bhutto, making Gilgit-Baltistan de facto a Province of Pakistan, although constitutionally it was not a part of Pakistan, but only an administered area.

Besides, there is a glaring contradiction between the Constitution of Pakistan and the Interim Constitution of Pakistan Administered Jammu & Kashmir Act, 1974. Article 257 states that the 'people of J&K are free to define their relationship with Pakistan if (and after) they decide to accede to Pakistan'. However, in terms of the Azad Jammu & Kashmir Interim Constitution Act of 1974,

> No person or political party in AJK is permitted to propagate against or take part in activities prejudicial or detrimental to the ideology of the State's accession to Pakistan. No person can assume office unless he/she takes the oath of Jammu and Kashmir's accession to Pakistan and nobody can be appointed to any government job unless he/she expresses loyalty to the concept of J & K's accession to Pakistan.
>
> ('Jammu and Kashmir—Paradise lost', 2019, braintoast.worldpress.com)

Thus, even though Pakistan has constitutionally provided special status to the State of J&K in Gilgit-Baltistan, the Government of Pakistan abrogated in 1974 the special status provided in the State Subject Rule. Similarly, Azad Kashmir is not *azad* (meaning free) in practice, since the Pakistani authorities govern the Azad Jammu & Kashmir government with tight controls on basic freedoms of AJK residents.

Framing of Article 370

Having decided to put an article in the Indian Constitution to take care of the promises made to the Maharaja at the time of accession to India under exceptional circumstances that have been discussed before in the previous chapter, the political leaders of Delhi and Kashmir joined hands to start framing that article.

Meanwhile, about three days after Kashmir's accession to India, Maharaja Hari Singh appointed Sheikh Abdullah to function as the Head of Administration with power to deal with the emergency, through an *Emergency Administration Order* on 30 October 1947. Further on 5 March 1948, the Maharaja, through a proclamation replaced the Emergency Administration by a *Popular Interim Government*. He also appointed a Council of Ministers with Sheikh Abdullah as the Prime Minister. On 9 June 1949, Maharaja Hari Singh entrusted Yuvraj Karan Singh with all the powers of Maharaja. It is said that Sheikh Abdullah was not very comfortable with Maharaja Hari Singh and he was happy with this handing over the charge to Yuvaraj Karan Singh.

Two developments of utmost importance were proceeding simultaneously. One was the *formulation of Article 370* to be considered by the Constituent Assembly of India, for inclusion in the Constitution of India and the other was the *proceedings in the freshly formed Constituent Assembly of Jammu & Kashmir for bringing out the Constitution of Jammu & Kashmir* under the changed circumstances. It may be recalled, the Princely State of Kashmir had its own Constitution since 1939 in terms of the J&K Constitution Act, 1939. But, that was a Royal Constitution securing more of the Maharaja's interest and hence inactive for quite some time.

On framing of the Constitution of India, on 16 June 1949, Sheikh Abdullah and his three other colleagues from the National Conference were chosen to represent Kashmir in the Constituent Assembly in Delhi. It further affirmed the integration of the State of Jammu & Kashmir with the

Constitution-making process in India, particularly in respect of framing of Article 370, *which was initially marked as Article 306A in the draft.*

Meanwhile, on 15 and 16 May 1949 there were important meetings at Sardar Patel's house at New Delhi between Pandit Nehru and his colleagues and Sheikh Abdullah and his colleagues regarding the future of Kashmir with reference to its relationship with Government of India, framing of the Constitution for Kashmir, etc. In response to certain issues raised by Sheikh Abdullah and his colleagues, Pandit Nehru wrote to him on 18 May 1949, after showing this to Sardar Patel, before issuing the same.

Nehru's letter to Sheikh Abdullah—issue-wise response
The relevant extracts of the letter which cover the subjects discussed during those two meetings and *Pandit Nehru's issue-wise responses,* which are self-explanatory, are quoted below:

2. Among the subjects that were discussed were: (i) the framing of a constitution for the State, (ii) the subjects in respect of which the State should accede to the Union of India, (iii) the monarchical form of government in the State, (iv) the control of the State Forces, and (v) the rights of the citizens of the State to equality of opportunity for service in the Indian Army.

3. As regards (i) and (iii), it has been the settled policy of the Government of India, which on many occasions has been stated both by Sardar

Patel and me, that the *constitution of Jammu and Kashmir State is a matter for determination by the people of the State represented in a Constituent Assembly convened for the purpose.* In the special circumstances of the State of Jammu and Kashmir, the Government of India have no objection to the Constituent Assembly of the State considering the question of the continuance of the association of the State with a constitutional monarchy.

4. In regard to (ii), Jammu and Kashmir State now stands acceded to the Indian Union in respect of three subjects, namely, Foreign Affairs, Defence and Communications. It will be for the Constituent Assembly of the State, when convened, to determine in respect of what other subjects the State may accede.

5. Regarding (iv), both the operational and administrative control over the State Forces has already, with the consent of the Government of Jammu and Kashmir State, been taken over by the Indian Army. The final arrangements in this connection, for the duration of the present emergency, including financial responsibility for the expenditure involved, were agreed to between us on the 16th inst.

6. As regards (v), the citizens of the State will have equality of opportunity for service in the Indian Army. Under Article 10 of the draft of the new Constitution, as passed by the Constituent

> Assembly of India, *equality of opportunity for employment under the State, including employment in the Indian Army, is declared to be amongst the fundamental rights of all Indian citizens.*

7. I trust that the Government of India's position, as stated above, will give you the clarification that you have asked for (Noorani 2014: 51).

In this letter, Pandit Nehru clearly stated that the State of Jammu and Kashmir stood acceded to the Indian Union in respect of three subjects namely, Foreign Affairs, Defence and Communications. He had further clarified that *it would be for the Constituent Assembly of the State of J&K, when convened, to determine in respect of what other subjects the State may accede.* Obviously, he was relying upon the Instrument of Accession dated 26 October 1947, signed by Maharaja Hari Singh and accepted by Governor General of India, Lord Mountbatten.

Chequered history of Article 370 (Draft Article 306A)

Initially, Article 370 was proposed as Draft Article 306A in the Constituent Assembly of India. It had a chequered history, largely due to difference of opinions between the leaders of India and those of Jammu & Kashmir. It may be clarified here, *while all matters relating to the framing of the Constitution were being discussed in the Constituent Assembly of the Indian Dominion, the matters relating to introduction of Article 370 into the Indian Constitution were being negotiated mainly between the leaders in Delhi and those of Jammu & Kashmir, and thereafter these were placed before the Constituent Assembly.*

After four members of the National Conference led by Sheikh Abdullah joined the Constituent Assembly on 16 June 1949, negotiations on framing of Article 370 (Draft Article 370) gathered steam. The Government of Jammu & Kashmir had proposed Article 306A in a certain form, some clauses of which were not accepted by the Ministry of States (Princely States) of the Government of India.

N. Gopalaswami's assertion regarding Nehru's statement

Meanwhile, during the Constitution Assembly debates on 27 May 1949 a doubt was raised by a learned Member of the Assembly about the correctness of Pandit Nehru's statement that Kashmir's accession to India was complete. *N. Gopalaswami Ayyangar (also referred to as N. Gopalaswami), Minister in charge of the States (Princely States)* in the Government of India, asserted that *Pandit Nehru's statement was correct.* N. Gopalaswami stated as follows:

> I maintain that it is perfectly correct. The accession was offered by the Maharaja and it was accepted by the Governor General of the time. I have a copy of that document before me. It is an absolutely unconditional offer … Now the correct position is this. The accession is complete. No doubt, we have offered to have a plebiscite taken when the conditions are created for the holding of a proper, fair and impartial plebiscite. But that *plebiscite is merely for the purpose of giving the people of the State the opportunity of expressing their will, and the expression of their will, will be*

only in the direction of whether they would ratify the accession that has already taken place—not ratify in the sense that that act of ratification is necessary for the completion of the accession, but if the plebiscite produces a verdict which is against the continuance of accession to India of the Kashmir State, then that we are committed to is simply this, *that we shall not stand in the way of Kashmir separating herself away from India.* In this connection, I should like to draw the attention of the House to the Provisions of the *Indian Independence Act* under which, when a State accedes and subsequently wishes to get out of the act of accession, thus separating itself from the main Dominion, it cannot do so except with the consent of the Dominion. Our commitment is simply this, that *if and when a plebiscite comes to be taken and if the verdict of that plebiscite is against India, then we shall not stand in the way of the wishes of the people of Kashmir being given effect to, if they want to go away from us.* That is all that it means. So I maintain that the statement that the accession at present is complete is a perfectly correct description of the existing state of things. (Noorani 2014: 54–6)

After protracted negotiations, *on 17 October 1949, N. Gopalaswami,* the Minister of States *presented Article 306A to be inserted after Article 306 of the Draft Constitution in the Constituent Assembly of India. Finally it became Article 370.*

Gopalaswami's exposition of Article 370 (Draft 306A)

In his detailed exposition of Art 306A (finally, Article 370), *N. Gopalaswami explained the reasons for the proposed special treatment to Kashmir.* The words 'states' and 'Indian States' used in his speech refer to the 'Princely States'. Relevant extracts of his speech, which are self-explanatory, are quoted below.

> *The accession took place on the 26th October, 1947. Since then, the State has had a chequered history. Conditions are not yet normal in the State. The meaning of this accession is that at present that State is a unit of a federal State, namely, the Dominion of India. This Dominion is getting transformed into a Republic, which will be inaugurated on the 26th January, 1950. The Jammu and Kashmir State, therefore, has to become a unit of the new Republic of India.*
>
> … in the case of practically all States, other than the State of Jammu and Kashmir, their constitutions also have been embodied in the Constitution for the whole of India. All those other States have agreed to integrate themselves in that way and accept the Constitution provided.
>
> … The discrimination is due to the special conditions of Kashmir. That particular State is not yet ripe for this kind of integration. It is the hope of everybody here that in due course even Jammu and Kashmir will become ripe for the same sort of integration as has taken place in the case of other

States. At present it is not possible to achieve that integration. There are various reasons why this is not possible now. I shall refer again to this a little later.

In the case of the other Indian States or Unions of States there are two or three points which have got to be remembered. They have all accepted the Constitution framed for States in Part I of the new Constitution and those provisions have been adapted so as to suit conditions of Indian States and Unions of States. Secondly, the Centre, that is the Republican Federal Centre will have power to make laws applying in every such State or Union to all Union and Concurrent Subjects. Thirdly, a uniformity of relationship has been established between those States and Unions and the Centre. Kashmir's conditions are, as I have said, special and require special treatment. (Noorani 2014: 66–7)

N. Gopalaswami continued to explain the special conditions in Kashmir, as distinct from the conditions in other Princely States. Extracts of his speech are quoted below.

In the first place, there has been a war going on within the limits of Jammu and Kashmir State.

There was a cease-fire agreed to at the beginning of this year and that cease-fire is still on. But the conditions in the State are still unusual and abnormal. They have not settled down. It is therefore necessary that the administration of the State should be geared to these unusual conditions until normal life is restored as in the case of the other States. Part of the State is still in the hands of rebels and enemies.

Again, the Government of India have committed themselves to the people of Kashmir in certain respects. They have committed themselves to the position that an opportunity would be given to the people of the State to decide for themselves whether they will remain with the Republic or wish to go out of it. We are also committed to ascertaining this will of the people by means of a plebiscite provided that peaceful and normal conditions are restored and the impartiality of the plebiscite could be guaranteed. We have also agreed that the will of the people, through the instrument of a constituent assembly, will determine the constitution of the State as well as the sphere of Union jurisdiction over the State.

At present, the legislature which was known as the Praja Sabha in the State is dead. Neither that legislature nor a constituent assembly can be convoked or can function until complete peace comes to prevail in that State. We have therefore to deal with the Government of the State which, as represented in its Council of Ministers, reflects the opinion of the largest political party in the State. Till a constituent assembly comes into being, only an interim arrangement is possible and not an arrangement which could at once be brought into line with the arrangement that exists in the case of the other States.

N. Gopalaswami concluded on the reasons for special treatment to Kashmir as follows. *'Now, if you remember the viewpoints that I have mentioned, it is an inevitable conclusion that, at the present moment, we could establish only an interim system. Article 306A is an attempt to establish such a system'* (Noorani 2014: 67–8).

Thereafter, N. Gopalaswami, proceeded to explain the provisions of Article 306A *(which was finally inserted in the Constitution as Article 370).*

Article 370 (Draft Article 306A)

Let us have a look at Article 370, which was presented in the Constituent Assembly as the draft Article 306A. The said article is reproduced below:

Temporary Provisions with Respect to the State of Jammu & Kashmir

370. (i) Notwithstanding anything in this Constitution:

(a) the provisions of Article 238 shall not apply in relation to the State of Jammu and Kashmir;

(b) the power of Parliament to make laws for the said State shall be limited to:

i. those matters in the Union List and the Concurrent List which, in consultation with the Government of the State, are declared by the President to correspond to matters specified in the Instrument of Accession governing the accession of the State to the Dominion of India as the matters with respect to which the Dominion Legislature may make laws for that State; and

ii. such other matters in the said Lists as, with the concurrence of the Government of the State, the President may by order specify.

Explanation:- For the purposes of this article, the Government of the State means the person for the time being recognized by the President as the Maharaja of Jammu and Kashmir acting on the advice of the Council of Ministers for the time being in office under the Maharaja's Proclamation dated the fifth day of March, 1948;

(c) the provisions of article I and of this article shall apply in relation to that State;

(d) such of the other provisions of this Constitution shall apply in relation to that State subject to such exceptions and modifications as the President may by order specify;

Provided that no such order which relates to the matters specified in the Instrument of Accession of the State referred to in paragraph (i) of sub–clause (b) shall be issued except in consultation with the Government of the State:

Provided further that no such order which relates to matters other than those referred to in the last preceding proviso shall be issued except with the concurrence of the Government.

(2) if the concurrence of the Government of the State referred to in paragraph (ii) of sub–clause

(b) of clause (I) or in the second proviso to sub–clause (d) of that clause be given before the Constituent Assembly for the purpose of framing the Constitution of the State is convened, it shall be placed before such Assembly for such decision as it may take thereon.

(3) Notwithstanding anything in the foregoing provisions of this article, the President may, by public notification, declare that this article shall cease to be operative or shall be operative only with such exceptions and modification and from such date as he may specify.

Provided that the recommendation of the Constituent Assembly of the State referred to in clause (2) shall be necessary before the President issues such a notification. (Noorani 2014: 79–81)

Final Impact of Article 370 read with Article 1

The final effect of the Article 370 read with Article 1 of the Constitution can be summarized as follows.

(a) The State of Jammu and Kashmir continues to be part of India. The act of accession was unequivocally given legal effect by *declaring Jammu & Kashmir a part of the territory of India by virtue of Article 1 read with Serial No. 15 of the First Schedule. Articles 1 and 370 are the only Articles of the Constitution of India which would apply of their own force to Jammu & Kashmir.*

(b) Article 238, which concerns application of certain provisions relating to the Princely States placed in Part B of the First Schedule of the Constitution, will have no effect on the State of Jammu & Kashmir, although this Princely State has been placed in Part B of the said Schedule.

(c) *The application of Articles other than Articles 1 and 370 was to be determined by the President of India in consultation with the Government of the State of J&K.*

(d) The legislative authority of Parliament over the State of J&K would be confined to those items of the Union and Concurrent Lists as correspond to *matters specified in the Instrument of Accession of the State of J&K.*

(e) As a corollary, in addition to Defence, External Affairs and Communication, which are specified in the Instrument of Accession of Kashmir, *the Union Parliament can also make laws with regard to the items in the Union and Concurrent Lists, but only with concurrence of the State Government.*

(f) In terms of *Clause (3) of Article 370*, the President of India may, *on the recommendations of the Constituent Assembly*, issue an order that the *Article 370 will either cease to be operative, or shall be operative only subject to such exceptions and modifications* as may be specified by the President. *But, before he issues any order of that kind, he must have the recommendation of the Constituent Assembly of Jammu & Kashmir.*

Article 370 and Article 1 explained by N. Gopalaswami

In order to understand and appreciate the foregoing observations on the Article 370 (draft Article 306A) read with Article 1, *extracts of the speech of N. Gopalaswami in the constituent Assembly are given below.* He first explained that Article 211 A *(Changed to Article 238* later) authorizes the application of the Constitution of India to all the Princely States (also called Indian States), *except the State Jammu & Kashmir, the only state that has its own constitution.* Thereafter, he dealt with the legislative authority of Parliament over the State of J & K as follows:

> *The Second portion of this article relates to the legislative authority of Parliament over the Jammu and Kashmir State. This is governed primarily by the Instrument of Accession. Broadly speaking, that legislative power is confined to the three subjects of defence, foreign affairs and communications, but as a matter of fact these broad categories include a number of items which are listed in the Instrument of Accession. I believe they number some twenty to twenty–five. Now, these items have undergone a change in description, in numbering, in arrangement, as amongst themselves, in List I and List III of the new Constitution. It is therefore necessary that the items mentioned in the Instrument of Accession should be brought into line with the changed designations of entries in Lists I and III of the new Constitution. So, clause (1) (b) of article 306A says that this listing of the items as per the terms of the new Constitution should be done by the President in consultation with the Government of the State.*
>
> *Clause (b) (ii) refers to possible additions to the List in the Instrument of Accession, and these additions could*

*be made according to the provisions of this article with
the concurrence of the Government of the State. The idea
is that even before the Constitution Assembly meets, it
may be necessary in the interests of both the Centre and
the State that certain items which are not included in the
Instrument of Accession would be appropriately added
to the List in the Instrument so that administration,
legislation and executive action might be furthered, and
as this may happen before the Constituent Assembly
meets, the only authority from whom we can get consent
for the addition is the Government of the State. That is
provided for.* (Noorani 2014: 68–9)

N. Gopalaswami's explanation of Clauses (c) & (d)

On the clauses (c) and (d) which refer to the provisions of the
Constitution other than the matters listed in Lists I and III, N.
Gopalaswami explained as follows:

*Clauses (c) and (d) refer to the provisions of the
Constitutions other than the matters listed in Lists I
and III. These various provisions have been divided
into certain categories. The first according to this draft
is that article 1 of the Constitution will automatically
apply. As you know,* it describes the territory of India,
and includes amongst these territories all the States
mentioned in Part III, and Jammu and Kashmir is
one of the States mentioned in Part III. With regard
to the other provisions in the Constitution, these will
apply to the Jammu and Kashmir State with such

exceptions and modifications as may be decided on when the President issues an Order to that effect. That Order can be issued in regard to subjects mentioned in the Instrument of Accession only after *consultation* with the Government of the State. In regard to other matters, the *concurrence* of that Government has to be taken. *(emphasis added)*

Now, it is not the case, nor is it the intention of the members of the Kashmir Government whom I took the opportunity of consulting before this draft was finalized—it is not their intention that the other provisions of the Constitution are not to apply. Their particular point of view is that these provisions should apply only in cases where they can suitably apply and only subject to such modifications or exceptions as the particular conditions of the Jammu and Kashmir State may require. I wish to say no more about that particular point at the present moment (Noorani 2014: 70).

N. Gopalaswami on 'Concurrence'

On Clause (2) that provides for the requirement of concurrence of the Government of Jammu & Kashmir, N. Gopalaswami clarified as follows:

Then we come to clause (2). You will remember that several of these clauses provide for the concurrence of the Government of Jammu and Kashmir State. Now, these relate particularly to matters which are not mentioned in the Instrument of Accession, and it is one of our commitments to the people and Government of Kashmir that no such additions should be made except with the consent of the Constituent Assembly which may be called in the State for the purpose of framing its Constitution. In order words, what we are committed to is that these additions are matters for the determination of the Constituent Assembly of the State (Noorani 2014: 70–1).

Summing up by N. Gopalaswami

Thereafter, while explaining Clause (3), the last clause which was meant for future exigencies, N. Gopalaswami summed up his detailed exposition of Article 370 (306A in the Draft) read with Article 238 (211 A in the Draft).

The extracts are quoted below:

The last clause refers to what may happen later on. We have said article 211A will not apply to the Jammu and Kashmir State. But that cannot be a permanent feature of the Constitution of the State, and hope it will not be. So the provision is made that when the Constituent Assembly of the State has met and taken its decision both on the Constitution for the State and on the range of federal jurisdiction over the State, the President may on the recommendation of that Constituent Assembly issue an order that this article 306A shall either cease to be operative, or shall be operative only subject to such exceptions and modifications as may be specified by him. But before he issues any order of that kind the recommendation of the Constituent Assembly will be a condition precedent. That explains the whole of this article.

The effect of this article is that the Jammu and Kashmir State which is now a part of India will continue to be a part of India, will be a unit of the future Federal Republic of India and the Union Legislature will get jurisdiction to enact laws on matters specified either in the Instrument of Accession or by later addition with the concurrence of the Government of the State. And steps have to be taken for the purpose of convening a Constituent Assembly in due course which will go into the matters I have already referred to. When it has come to a decision on the different matters it will make a recommendation to the President who will either abrogate article 306A or direct that it shall apply with such modifications and exceptions as the Constituent Assembly may recommend. That, Sir, is briefly a description of the effect of this article, and I hope the House will carry it (Noorani 2014: 71–2).

At the end of the foregoing exposition of Article 370 (306A in the Draft), the Draft Article 306A was adopted without a vote in the Constituent Assembly on 17 October 1949.

Yuvraj's Proclamation

Yuvraj Karan Singh made a proclamation on 25 November 1949 accepting the new Constitution as drafted by the Constituent

Assembly. By this proclamation, the Yuvaraj, inter alia, declared and directed that the Indian Constitution will govern the constitutional relationship between the State of Jammu & Kashmir and the Union of India and it will be enforced in the State of J&K by him, his heirs and successors in accordance with the tenor of its provisions. He also ordered that the provisions of the said Constitution will supersede and abrogate all other existing constitutional provisions inconsistent therewith.

President's First Order of 1950

The next important thing to happen was the President of India's First order under Article 370, applying the Indian Constitution to the State of Jammu & Kashmir on 26 January 1950 (Jagmohan 1994: 232; Noorani 2014: 80–6). This order called the Constitution (Application to Jammu and Kashmir) Order, 1950, specifies the matters in the First Schedule to the order, with regard to which alone the Indian Parliament can make laws for the States. Further, the order specifies that besides Article 1 and 370, the only other provisions that can apply to the State of J&K will be those specified in the Second Schedule to this order.

Difficulties in carrying Article 370 through

While still on Article 370, it would be necessary to mention that it was not so easy for the Government of India to carry through the passing of Article 370 in the Constituent Assembly because of certain contra views on the text of the Draft Article 306A (which later became Article 370, when passed), from Sheikh Abdullah and other leaders of the National Conference.

Instead of going into the details of these, suffice it to say that the Draft Article 306A as proposed by the Government of Jammu & Kashmir was not accepted by the Ministry of States of the Government of India led by N. Gopalaswami and there were follow-up discussions between him and Sheikh Abdullah and his team. Gopalaswami had kept Sardar Patel informed on these matters of disagreement. After Gopalaswami moved the Final Draft of Article 306A on 17 October 1949 and made a detailed exposition of the Article, the Draft Article 306A was adopted without a vote.

Later, Sheikh Abdullah in his letter to N. Gopalaswami on 17 October 1949, the same day that the Draft Article 306A was adopted, complained of certain alterations of Article 370 made unilaterally, without discussing with them again. However, Gopalaswami in his reply dated 18 October 1949, addressed to Sheikh Abdullah, maintained that the changes were in keeping with his ongoing talks with Sheikh Abdullah and his colleagues.

During this period Pandit Nehru was away. So, Sardar Patel wrote to Nehru on 3 November 1949 informing him about the changed draft 306A that N. Gopalaswami had placed in the Constituent Assembly, and also that

> Sheikh Sahib has not reconciled himself to the change, but we could not accommodate him in this matter and the provision was passed through the House as we had modified. After this he wrote a letter to Gopalaswami Ayyangar threatening to resign from the membership of the Constituent Assembly. Gopalaswami has replied

asking him to defer his decision until you returned. (Noorani 2014: 77)

The matter must have been sorted out after Pandit Nehru's return and further action thereafter.

Article 370 together with Amendment in 'Explanation':

370. Temporary provisions with respect to the State of Jammu and Kashmir.—(1) Notwithstanding anything in this Constitution,—

(a) the provisions of article 238 shall not apply in relation to the State of Jammu and Kashmir;

(b) the power of Parliament to make laws for the said State shall be limited to—

(i) those matters in the Union List and the Concurrent List which, in consultation with the Government of the State, are declared by the President to correspond to matters specified in the Instrument of Accession governing the accession of the State to the Dominion of India as the matters with respect to which the Dominion Legislature may make laws for that State; and

(ii) such other matters in the said Lists as, with the concurrence of the Government of the State, the President may by order specify.

Explanation.—For the purposes of this article,

the Government of the State means the person for the time being recognised by the President as the Maharaja of Jammu and Kashmir acting on the advice of the Council of Ministers for the time being in office under the Maharaja's Proclamation dated the fifth day of March, 1948;

(c) the provisions of article 1 and of this article shall apply in relation to that State;

(d) such of the other provisions of this Constitution shall apply in relation to that State subject to such exceptions and modifications as the President may by order to specify:

Provided that no such order which relates to the matters specified in the Instrument of Accession of the State referred to in paragraph (i) of sub-clause (b) shall be issued except in consultation with the Government of the State:

Provided further that no such order which relates to matters other than those referred to in the last preceding proviso shall be issued except with the concurrence of that Government.

(2) If the concurrence of the Government of the State referred to in paragraph (ii) of sub-clause (b) of clause (1) or in the second proviso to sub-clause (d) of that clause be given before the Constituent Assembly for the purpose of framing the Constitution of the State is convened, it shall be placed before such Assembly for such decision as it may take thereon.

(3) Notwithstanding anything in the foregoing provisions of this article, the President may, by public notification, declare that this article shall cease to be operative or shall be operative only with such exceptions and modifications and from such date as he may specify:

Provided that the recommendation of the Constituent Assembly of the State referred to in clause (2) shall be necessary before the President issues such a notification

Amendment effective from 17 November 1952

1. In exercise of the powers conferred by this article the President, on the recommendation of the Constituent Assembly of the State of Jammu and Kashmir, declared that, as from the 17th day of November, 1952, the said Art. 370 shall be operative with the modification that for the Explanation in cl. (1) thereof, the following Explanation is substituted, namely:-

'Explanation.– For the purposes of this article, the Government of the State means the person for the time being recognised by the President on the recommendation of the Legislative Assembly of the State as the *Sadar-i-riyasat* of Jammu and Kashmir, acting on the advice of the Council of Ministers of the State for the time being in office.' (Ministry of Law Order No. C.O. 44, dated the 15th November, 1952). *Now 'Governor' (Noorani 2014: 225).

New Constituent Assembly for Kashmir

In early January 1951, the All J&K National Conference resolved to convene the Constituent Assembly for framing a fresh Constitution for the State. It may be recalled, the Princely State of J&K did have a Constitution in 1939. But, it was basically Maharaja-centric and it did not work.

After the said resolution, Sheikh Abdullah had some serious and frank discussions with C. Rajagopalachari, then Union Home Minister, Maulana Abul Kalam Azad and N. Gopalaswami on the setting up the Constituent Assembly. On 16 January 1951, Sheikh Abdullah had written a letter to N. Gopalaswami, following up on those discussions. Though there were some disagreements on certain issues, those were sorted out. As mentioned before, on 1 May 1951, Yuvraj Karan Singh issued the proclamation convening Jammu & Kashmir's Constituent Assembly. It met for the first time on 31 October 1951.

Sheikh Abdullah's speech to the Constituent Assembly of Kashmir

The next event of importance was Sheikh Abdullah's Speech to the Constituent Assembly for Kashmir on 5 November 1951. In this lengthy speech he started by expressing his resolve to deliver a 'New Kashmir' through wise deliberations in the Constituent Assembly about the future of Kashmir. Some of his opening remarks are placed below:

> We meet here today, in this palace hall, once the symbol of unquestioned monarchial authority, as free citizens of the New Kashmir for which we have

so long struggled. I see about me in this hall, many companions—Hindus, Muslims, Buddhists, Harijans and Sikhs, who first trod with me that path which has brought us to this Constituent Assembly of 1951.

We must remember that our struggle for power has now reached its successful climax in the convening of this Constituent Assembly. It is for you to translate the vision of New Kashmir into reality, and I would remind you of its opening words, which will inspire our labours. (Noorani 2014: 97–8)

Thereafter, Sheikh Abdullah dealt with the main functions that the Constituent Assembly would be called upon to perform. He also explained Kashmir's constitutionalities with India. In this context, he spoke on the merits and demerits of the three choices that Kashmir had—joining India or joining Pakistan or remaining independent like being the Switzerland of the East. Finally, he explained that *joining India was the best choice.*

Differences between Nehru and Sheikh Abdullah

As the process of Constitution making for the State of J&K was in progress in right earnest, both Pandit Nehru and Sheikh Abdullah were concerned about settling all pending disputes between the Government of India and the State Government of J&K. But, there was a difference in their approaches. *Pandit Nehru was keen on securing Kashmir's closer integration with the rest of India, while Sheikh Abdullah's priority was to preserve Kashmir's autonomy.*

Delhi Agreement

On 20 July 1952, Pandit Nehru along with the Foreign Affairs Committee of the Cabinet met Sheikh Abdullah, the 'Prime Minister' of Jammu & Kashmir along with his colleagues, which included Bakshi Ghulam Mohammad, Mirza Afzal Beg and D.P. Dhar. The outcome of the said meeting, famously known as the *Delhi Agreement* was recorded in Nehru's Note on discussions with Kashmir's Delegation on 20 July 1952. The principal points that were taken up for discussion were as follows:

(a) Head of the State – definition;

(b) Citizenship – determination;

(c) Fundamental Rights – their extent;

(d) Supreme Court – jurisdiction;

(e) National Flag alongside the State Flag;

(f) President of India – certain powers;

(g) Financial Integration – the Principle;

(h) Emergency Powers – Application of Articles 352, 356 or 360 of the Constitution;

(Noorani 2014: 133)

Pandit Nehru announced the Delhi Agreement through a Statement in the Parliament on 24 July 1952 (Noorani 2014: 138).

Sheikh Abdullah placed the Agreement in the J&K Constituent Assembly on 11 August 1952, and asked the J&K Constituent Assembly to endorse the Delhi Agreement on 14 August 1952 (Noorani 2014: 158).

Article 35A—Link with the Kashmir State Constitution

Before proceeding further with the making of the Constitution for Kashmir, let us examine the provisions of *Article 35A* of the Constitution of India. An interesting aspect of Article 35A is that if one searches for it in the Indian Constitution after Article 35, one will not find it there, and instead Article 36 would come after Article 35. Article 35A does not appear in the main body of the Constitution; instead it is listed in Appendix I of the Constitution.

Article 35A stemmed out of Article 370

In terms of Article 370 (1) (c) and (d),

> Notwithstanding anything in this Constitution,
> (c) the provisions of Article 1 and of this Article shall apply in relation to that State;
> (d) *such of the other provisions of this Constitution shall apply in relation to that State subject* to such exception... *(emphasis added)*.

Presidential Order of 1954

In terms of the Delhi Agreement of 1952 between the leaders of the Congress and National Conference, certain rights like Indian Citizenship were to be extended to State subjects in Kashmir, while certain others were to be restricted to Kashmiris alone, considering Kashmir's special status. Thus was issued the Presidential Order under Article 370(1)(d) titled '*The Constitution (Application to Jammu and Kashmir) Order 1954 dated May 14, 1954*' (Noorani 2014: 264); in a unique way.

Article 35A was inserted in the Indian Constitution through this Presidential Order, instead of the more common way of Amendment of the Constitution through Parliament.

The aforesaid Presidential Order clearly stated in the beginning that this order was passed by the President in exercise of the powers conferred by clause (1) of Article 370 of the Constitution, with the concurrence of the Government of the State of Jammu & Kashmir.

Thereafter, the said order stated that in addition to Article 1 and Article 370, certain other provisions of the Constitution of India will apply in relation to the State of J&K, and those were laid down in that Order.

In Part III, Clause (j) of the said order, we find the birth of article 35A. Article 35A empowers the Jammu & Kashmir Legislature to do a few things including defining 'Permanent Residents' of the State, and emphasizing exclusive and special rights and privileges with regard to acquisition of immovable property in the State, employment under the State Government, etc.

Having been thus empowered by virtue of the previously mentioned Instrument of Accession and Article 370, the State of J&K got empowered to decree exceptions to the extension of Indian Constitution to the State in certain areas. Thus, *Article 35A can be said to be an exception authorized by the Article 370, clause (1) (d).*

For illustration, the Constitution of Jammu & Kashmir that came into force on 17 November 1956 put some restriction on acquiring land and property in Kashmir and gave that right only to the Permanent Residents.

Text of Article 35A

The text of Article 35A of the Constitution of India appears on the following pages:

Article 35 A. Saving of law with respect to permanent residents and their rights:-
Notwithstanding anything contained in this Constitution, no existing law in force in the State of Jammu and Kashmir, and no law hereafter enacted by the Legislature of the State:

(a) defining the classes or persons who are, or shall be permanent residents of the State of Jammu & Kashmir or,

(b) conferring on such permanent residents any special rights and privileges or imposing upon other persons any restrictions as respects:-

i   employment under the State Government;

ii   acquisition of immovable property in the State;

iii settlement in the State; or

iv   right to scholarship and such other forms of aid as the State Government may provide, shall be void on the ground that is inconsistent with or takes away or abridges any rights conferred on the other citizens of India by any provision of this part. (Noorani 2014: 268)

Sections 6 to 10 of the Constitution of the State of Jammu & Kashmir

While the main features of the Constitution of Jammu & Kashmir will be discussed later in this chapter, the *Sections 6 to 10 of the J&K Constitution* that relate to Permanent Residents of Kashmir has a direct link with *Article 35A* of the Indian Constitution and therefore these five Sections are being discussed here, for the sake of convenience of understanding. The text of Sections 6 to 10 appears below.

Part III: Permanent Residents

Permanent Residents

6. (1) Every person who is, or is deemed to be, a citizen of India under the provisions of the Constitution of India shall be a permanent resident of the State, if on the fourteenth day of May, 1954:

a.   he was a State Subject of Class I or of Class II; or

b.   having lawfully acquired immovable property in the State, he has been ordinarily resident in the State for not less than ten years prior to that date.

2.   Any person who, before the fourteenth day of May, 1954 was a State Subject of Class I or of Class II and who, having migrated after the first day of March, 1947, to the territory now included in Pakistan, returns to the state under a permit for resettlement in the State or for permanent return issued by or under the authority or any law made by the State Legislature shall on such return be a permanent resident of the State.

3. In this section, the expression 'State Subject of Class I or of Class II' shall have the same meaning as in State Notification No. I-L/84 dated the twentieth April, 1927, read with State Notification No. 13/L dated the twenty-seventh June, 1932.

Construction of References to State Subject in the Existing Laws

7. Unless the context otherwise requires, all references in any existing law to hereditary State Subjects or to State Subject of Class I or of Class II or of Class III shall be construed as references to permanent residents of the State.

Legislature to Define Permanent Residents

8. Nothing in the foregoing provisions of this Part shall derogate from the power of the State Legislature to make any law defining the classes of persons who are, or shall be, permanent residents of the State.

Special Provisions for Bills Relating to Permanent Residents

9. A Bill making provision for any of the following matters, namely:-

a. defining or altering the definition of, the classes of persons who are, or shall be, permanent residents of the State;

b. conferring on permanent residents any special rights or privileges;

c. regulating or modifying any special rights or privileges enjoyed by permanent residents; shall be deemed to be passed by either House of the Legislature only if it is passed by a majority of not less than two-thirds of the total membership of that House.

10. Rights of the Permanent Residents

The permanent residents of the State shall have all the rights guaranteed to them under the Constitution of India (Noorani 2014: 292–3).

A brief discussion on Article 35A and Sections 6 to 10

The main effect of these sections is that the Constitution of Jammu & Kashmir defined a 'Permanent Resident' (PR) of the State as a person who was a state subject on 14 May 1954, the date of the aforesaid Presidential Order, or who has been a resident of the State for 10 years prior to enforcement of this provision and has 'lawfully acquired immovable property in the State'.

Further, Article 35A gave certain benefits only to the 'Permanent Residents' of Kashmir such as employment in the State Government, acquisition of immovable property, settlement in the State, scholarship and other government aid. In fact, these benefits were just the continuation of pre-existing laws during the regime of Maharaja Hari Singh. The idea was that the benefits to which the residents of the erstwhile Princely State of Kashmir were entitled were not to be withdrawn with Kashmir joining the Indian Union.

Thus, it can be said that *Article 35A was the consequence of the autonomy given to the State of J&K under Article 370.*

Political developments

We now come back to certain political developments during the Constitution-making process for Kashmir. By early 1950, it started dawning in the minds of the people who matter that the National Conference had begun breaking into two camps on the issue of integration of Kashmir, one led by Sheikh Abdullah and Mirza Afzal Beg who advocated maximum distance from India within the terms of Article 370, and the other comprising Bakshi Ghulam Mohammad, G.M. Sadiq, D.P. Dhar, etc., who worked for greater integration with India. By the middle of 1950, Sheikh Abdullah revealed his thoughts when he started hinting at the option of independence of Kashmir to Sir Owen Dixon, the UN representative. He even started talking openly that Delhi should not advise him on matters outside Defence, External Affairs and Communications. As Prime Minister of India, Nehru could not ignore the words and actions of Sheikh Abdullah, his great friend so far. Nehru was in a dilemma. In May 1950, he wrote to his sister Vijaylakshmi Pandit, 'The most difficult thing in life is what to do with one's friends' (Guha 2008: 244).

Sheikh Abdullah's conflict with Indian leaders increased by April 1952, when he opposed Gopalaswami's attempt to extend the jurisdiction of the Comptroller and Auditor General of India to Kashmir.

In early May 1953, Sheikh Abdullah met Adlai Stevenson, an American leader of the Democratic Party and thereafter had a few more meetings with him. This fuelled rumors about his seeking Anglo-American support for Kashmir's independence. On 13 July, Martyrs' Day, he said in his speech, 'Kashmir should have the sympathy of both India and Pakistan. It is not necessary that our State should become an appendage of either India or Pakistan' (Akbar 1991: 149).

Arrest of Sheikh Abdullah

While Nehru was losing his patience with Sheikh Abdullah, the split in the National Conference on the issue of integration with India became quite open. An intelligence input that Sheikh Abdullah was trying to establish contact secretly with a representative of Pakistan helped Nehru to firm up his decision. On the evening of 8 August 1953, Dr Karan Singh, the *Sadar-i-Riyasat* dismissed Sheikh Abdullah and invited Bakshi Ghulam Mohammed to form the Government, and by midnight Dr Karan Singh ordered the arrest of Sheikh Abdullah. Bakshi Ghulam Mohammed took over the charge of Prime Minister of J & K on 9 August 1953.

Constitution of J&K—Main Features with a bearing on Article 370

Meanwhile, the Draft Constitution, as settled by the Drafting Committee, was introduced in early October, 1956. *The Constitution of J&K was finally enacted on 17 November 1956 and it came into force on 26 January 1957,* exactly seven years after the Constitution of India came into force on 26 January 1950.

A few main features of the Constitution of J&K, particularly those which have a bearing on Article 370 are mentioned below:

Section 3 on *Relationship of the State with the Union of India,* states:

'3. The State of Jammu and Kashmir is said and shall be an integral part of the Union of India' (Noorani 2014: 291).

In terms of *Section 4* on *Territory of the State*, 'the territory of the State shall comprise all the territories which on the fifteenth day of August, 1947, were under the sovereignty or suzerainty of the Ruler of State' (Noorani 2014: 291). Thus it has been made clear that the State of Jammu & Kashmir will include Pakistan Occupied Kashmir on the western border, Gilgit and Baltistan in the north-west and the north of Kashmir—both occupied by Pakistan, and Aksai Chin, presently occupied by China.

Section 5 states that '*the executive and legislative power of the State extended to all matters except those with respect to which Parliament has power to make laws for the State under the provisions of the Constitution of India*' (Noorani 2014: 292).

As explained while discussing Article 35A earlier in this chapter, *Sections 6 to 10 deal with various aspects related to Permanent Residents.* Out of these, Sections 6, 8 and 10 are of particular importance.

Section 6 broadly lays down the conditions to be qualified as Permanent Residents:

Section 8 authorizes the Legislature to *Define who are the Permanent Residents.*

Section 10 makes it clear that the Permanent *Residents* of the State shall have all the rights guaranteed to them under the Constitution of India.

Sections 26 to 34 deal with various subjects related to the Sadar-i-Riyasat, the *Head of State.*

Section 35 to 40 deal with the *Council of Ministers* to aid and advise the *Sadar-i-Riyasat*, Appointment of Ministers, etc.

Section 48 deals with Provision Relating to Pakistan Occupied Territory. It has been provided in the Section that notwithstanding anything contained in Section 47, until the area of the State under the occupation of Pakistan ceases to be so occupied and the people residing in that area elect their representatives, 25 seats in the Legislative Assembly shall remain vacant and shall not be taken into account for reckoning the total membership of the Assembly. Further, the said areas shall be excluded in delimiting the territorial constituencies under Section 47.

Constitutional Position of Kashmir in relation to Union of India (Before 5 August 2019)

In light of the special provisions of Article 370, it would be useful to summarize the salient features of the Constitutional position of the State of Jammu & Kashmir in relation to the Union of India, before certain provisions of Article 370 and Article 35A were abrogated on 5 and 6 August 2019.

First, as for the jurisdiction of Parliament in relation to Jammu & Kashmir, it got confined to the matters enumerated in the Union List and a few specified matters in the Concurrent List. Thus, while the residuary power of legislation belonged to the Parliament for all other States of India that residual power, excepting certain specified matters, belonged to the Legislature of the State of J&K.

Second, with regard to the *Autonomy of the State,* the plenary power of the Indian Parliament has been curbed in respect of certain matters where the Parliament cannot make any law without the consent of the J&K State Legislature. Similar fetters have been imposed upon the executive power of the Union to safeguard the autonomy of Kashmir; other states do not have this privilege. One can say that the federal relationship between the Union and the State of J&K respects the rights of the State more than in the case of other States of the Union.

Third, *no alteration of the area or boundaries* of the State of J&K can be made by Parliament *without the consent of the Legislature* of the State of J&K. *This provision is relevant in the present context, after 5 August 2019.*

Fourth, the provisions of the Indian Constitution relating to the *Directive Principles* do not apply to the State of J&K.

Fifth, the provisions of *Article 19* that deal with '*Right to Freedom of Speech and Expression*', '*Right to reside and settle in any part of the Territory*', etc., were made subject to special restrictions for a period of 25 years.

In this context, it is pointed out that some special rights regarding *employment, acquisition of property* and settlement, etc., were conferred on '*permanent residents*' of the State of J&K by inserting a new article—*Article 35A.*

Sixth, very importantly, Jammu & Kashmir was the only state to have its own *separate Constitution.* To elaborate, the Constitution of all States other than J&K is laid down in the Indian Constitution in Part–VI of the Constitution of India; but Kashmir had its own Constitution.

Seventh, the provisions of *Article 368* of the Constitution of India that deal with the *Power of Parliament to amend the*

Constitution and Procedure, therefore, were not applicable for the amendment of the State Constitution of Jammu & Kashmir. An act of Parliament is required for the amendment of any of the provisions of the Constitution of India. But, because of *Article 370*, the provisions of the State Constitution of J&K, (excepting those relating to the relationship of the State of J&K with the Union of India may be amended by an Act of Legislative Assembly of the State, by a majority of not less than two-thirds of the membership. Of course, there were certain other conditions and restrictions on such amendment. Another important aspect was that no amendment of the Constitution of India shall extend to Jammu & Kashmir unless it is so extended by an order of the President under Art 370(1) of the Constitution of India.

Eighth, the jurisdiction of Central Government institutions can be extended to the State of J&K by amendments of the Constitution Order. In fact, it has been done on quite a few occasions in the past few years in respect of jurisdiction of Comptroller and Auditor General, Election Commission, Special Leave Jurisdiction of the Supreme Court, etc.

Continuous dilution of Article 370

In view of the provisions of Article 370, an amendment made to the Constitution of India did not apply to the State of J&K, unless the amendment was made applicable to the State by a Presidential Order. The Presidential Order, again, could be issued only with the concurrence of the State Assembly/ State Government. The idea was to keep the autonomy of the State intact for the agreed subjects.

However, over the years, Article 370 has been hollowed out by making more and more provisions of the Indian Constitution applicable to the State of Jammu & Kashmir. The route was through the aforesaid Presidential Orders by using the provisions of the same Article 370. During the period from its introduction on 26 January 1957 and until its abrogation on 5 and 6 August 2019, there were 44 amendments; of course, these amendments were brought with the concurrence of the J&K State Legislature. A few of the amendments in particular, such as the extension of the authority of the Supreme Court over Kashmir were well appreciated by Sheikh Abdullah himself.

In the context of continuous hollowing out of Article 370, Gulzari Lal Nanda, then Home Minister said in December 1964, 'the provision enabling the President to issue orders was later converted into a tunnel in the wall'. But, even though the core of Article 370 was eroded much before 5 and 6 August 2019, the special status extended to the Kashmiris through Article 370 became a great emotive and sensitive issue for them. The debate whether the special status extended to Kashmir is temporary or permanent has also been going on, and this will be discussed later.

Concluding comments on the birth of Articles 370 and 35A

It would be clear that when the constitutional relationship between India and the State of Jammu & Kashmir was to be documented, there was a requirement of enshrining the elements of autonomy, some which were even put in the

Instrument of Accession, in the Constitution of India. It may be recalled, Kashmir did have its own Constitution since 1939, which was of course the King's Constitution all the way, and not of the people of Kashmir. The 'Naya Kashmir' of Sheikh Abdullah wanted a new and modern constitution. All these factors led the leaders in Delhi and those in Kashmir to include a suitable article enshrined in the Constitution of India that will ensure a 'special status' to Kashmir in terms of its accession to India.

That is how Article 370 and later Article 35A had their birth on 26 January 1950 and 14 May 1954, respectively. These two articles were to take care of the restricted autonomy for Kashmir. Article 35A, in particular, protected the demographic status of the J&K State in its prescribed constitutional form. These elements of Autonomy were also enshrined in the new Constitution of the State of J&K, which was introduced in November 1956.

CHAPTER-IV

Abolition of the Special Status of Article 370

Momentous decisions of 5 and 6 August 2019

Before spelling out the momentous decisions of 5 and 6 August 2019, it would be necessary to understand Article 370 and Article 35A as they stood before 5 August 2019. Article 370 had barred application of certain provisions of the Indian Constitution to the people of the State of Jammu and Kashmir; in other words, Article 370 limited the application of the provisions of the Indian Constitution to the State of Jammu & Kashmir.

Article 370(1)(c) and 370(1)(d) deal with the applicability of the Indian Constitution to the State of J&K. In terms of Article 370(1)(c), the two articles i.e. Article 1 and Article 370 of the Constitution will apply to J&K. Article 370(1)(d) is very important. Under this article, the Indian constitutional provisions could be applied to the State of J&K from time to time, as modified by the President through a Presidential Order and, importantly, after the concurrence of the State Government.

However, the most important provision of *Article 370* was the proviso to Clause 3. This clause itself authorized the President to pass an order removing or modifying parts of Article 370. But, there is an equally important 'proviso' to it;

the proviso stated: 'Provided that the recommendation of the Constituent Assembly of the State referred to in Clause (2) shall be necessary before the President issues such a notification'.

Thus, the recommendation of the Constituent Assembly of J&K was an essential requirement for Article 370 itself to be amended. The problem is that the Constituent Assembly of J&K was dissolved and it ceased to function from January 1957. This led to a longstanding debate on whether Article 370 has become permanent effectively, because there was no Constituent Assembly to give consent. Question has also been raised whether it would require a revival of the J&K State Constituent Assembly to amend it, or whether it can be amended through the normal amendment procedure under the Constitution.

In the present context, another important article is Article 367 which basically provides various guidelines about how the Constitution may be interpreted. Article 367 is the interpretation clause of the Constitution. The Presidential Order of 5 August 2019 added clause (4) with four sub-clauses to Article 367, in terms of which *'Sadar-i-Riyasat' will be construed as 'Governor of Jammu & Kashmir';* and the phrase *'State Government' shall include the Governor. Further, the words 'Constituent Assembly' used in Article 370(3) must be read as 'Legislative Assembly of Jammu & Kashmir'.*

Momentous decisions

Armed with these legal provisions, the Government of India proceeded to act on 5 and 6 August 2019, as follows:

First, the President of India, in exercise of the powers conferred by Clause (1) of Article 370 of the Constitution, issued the Constitution (Application to Jammu and Kashmir) Order, 2019, C.O. 272. By this Presidential Order, the 'special status' of Jammu and Kashmir in respect of certain provisions in the Indian Constitution was withdrawn. While Article 370 of the Indian constitution had barred application of certain provisions of the Indian Constitution to the people of the State of Jammu and Kashmir, the said Presidential Order of 5 August 2019 extended all provisions of the Constitution of India to Jammu and Kashmir.

In order to meet certain requirements, the said Presidential Order C.O. 272 first used the authority of Article 370(1) to amend a separate Constitutional provision i.e. Article 367 and added a fourth clause to Article 367 to expand the coverage of the expressions 'concurrence of the State General', 'concurrence of J&K State Constituent Assembly', etc. Details will be explained soon.

So, contrary to the public perception, *Article 370 of the Indian Constitution was not scrapped lock, stock and barrel; rather Article 370(1) has been used to withdraw the 'special status' previously extended to Jammu & Kashmir.*

Second, *Article 35A of the Indian Constitution became unconstitutional* by virtue of the aforesaid Presidential Order dated 5 August, 2019. It may be recalled that Article 35A had stemmed out of Article 370 and was in fact the consequence of the autonomy given to Kashmir through Article 370. Consequently, *certain special rights relating to land and property, employment etc., hitherto enjoyed by the 'Permanent Residents' in Kashmir were also rendered no longer valid.*

Third, by applying the new interpretation of Article 370(3) the 'Constituent Assembly' was replaced by the words 'Legislative Assembly of J&K'. But J&K was under President's Rule and there was no Legislative Assembly. Therefore it fell upon the Parliament to make a recommendation with regard to abrogating the special rights and privileges of the State of J&K, provided by Article 370. Accordingly, the recommendation of the Parliament to the President was issued by the Home Minister through a Resolution.

First resolution of Parliament

The *first statutory resolution in Parliament* to remove the special rights and privileges of the State of Jammu & Kashmir stated:

> That this House recommends the following public notification to be issued by the President of India under Article 370(3): 'In exercise of the powers conferred by Clause (3) of Article 370 read with clause (1) of Article 370 of the Constitution of India, the President, on the recommendation of the Parliament, is pleased to declare that, as from 5th of August, 2019, all clauses of the said Article 370 shall cease to be operative except clause (1)'.

Thus remained only Clause (1) of Article 370, and the rest abrogated. It can be said that Article 370 will survive on paper as:

> All provisions of this Constitution, as amended from time to time, without any modifications

or exceptions, shall apply to the State of Jammu and Kashmir notwithstanding anything contrary contained in *Article 152 or Article 308* or any other article of this Constitution or any other provision of the Constitution of Jammu and Kashmir or any law, document, judgment, ordinance, order, bye-law, rule, regulation, notification, custom or usage having the force of law in the territory of India, or any other instrument, treaty or agreement as envisaged under *Article 363* or otherwise.

Fourth, by virtue of the **Jammu and Kashmir Reorganisation Act, 2019,** passed by the Parliament, the State of J&K was divided into two parts—Jammu & Kashmir and Ladakh; both units were turned into two Union Territories—Jammu & Kashmir with a Legislature, similar to Puducherry, and Ladakh without any legislature, similar to Chandigarh. Thus, effectively both these territories will be under the direct control of the Central Government.

The above said Act states that the provisions contained in *Article 239A* of the Constitution that are applicable to the Union Territory of Puducherry will also apply to the Union Territory of Jammu & Kashmir. Through Article 239A of the Constitution, the UT of J & K will have a Legislative Assembly to enact laws on certain subjects and it will have a Council of Ministers headed by a Chief Minister to aid and advise the Lieutenant Governor on subjects related to such legislation. For the subjects outside the purview of the Assembly, the Lt. Governor does not need the aid and advice of the Chief Minister.

Thus, the Assembly of the Union Territory of the J & K will have the power to enact laws on matters under the State List and Concurrent List, except for the subjects that are exclusively under the ambit of the Union Government.

The above said Act also states that the Assembly can make laws on any subjects in the State and Concurrent Lists, except on state subjects relating to '*Public Order*' and '*Police*'. Thus, like in Delhi, all laws on these two subjects will be directly under the Centre.

As for the jurisdiction of the Assembly of the Union Territory of J&K, the subjects like land rights, land tenures, land improvement and transfer of agricultural land., etc. will be under the ambit of the Legislative Assembly. The All India Services and Anti-corruption Bureau will be under the jurisdiction of the Lt. Governor. Therefore, all appointments and other administrative matters relating to the Anti-corruption Bureau, CBI, will be directly under the Lt. Governor. Similarly, the Service matters including the matters relating to transfer and posting of officers will be within the jurisdiction of the Lt. Governor of the UT of J&K. Further, the Lt. Governor will make rules on the advice of the Council of Ministers for the allocation of business to the Ministers that will include the procedure to be adopted in case of difference of opinion between the Lt. Governor and the Council of Ministers or a Minister.

Thus, the J&K Assembly would be like Delhi in some respects and unlike Delhi in other aspects. To put it in a different way, the control of the Centre through the Lt. Governor over the Union Territory of Jammu & Kashmir would be more prominent and clearly defined.

Second resolution of Parliament

The second resolution said that the President has referred the *Jammu and Kashmir Reorganisation Bill, 2019* to the House 'under the proviso to Article 3 of the Constitution of India for its views as this House is vested with the powers of the State Legislature of Jammu and Kashmir, as per proclamation of the President of India dated 19th December, 2018'.

The Bill and the statutory resolutions were tabled by the Union Home Minister after the President signed the official notification 'The Constitution (Application to Jammu and Kashmir) Order, 2019', superseding 'The Constitution (Application to Jammu and Kashmir) Order, 1954' under which the Indian Constitution was applied only selectively to the State.

The said official notification clearly stated 'All the provisions of the Constitution, as amended from time to time, shall apply in relation to the state of Jammu and Kashmir...'

Three important documents

Thus, the important documents related to the recent Constitutional changes in respect of Article 370 and bifurcation of the State of Jammu & Kashmir are:

i   Presidential Order C.O. 272 that inter alia also amends Article 367;

ii   First Statutory Resolution of Parliament that recommends that the President removes the special status of Kashmir provided through Article 370, and thereby abrogate much of Article 370;

iii Second Statutory Resolution of Parliament in respect of Jammu & Kashmir Reorganisation Bill, 2019, by virtue of which the State of J&K was divided into two parts—Jammu & Kashmir and Ladakh.

Effect on Article 35A of the Presidential Order of August 2019

In light of the recent Presidential Order of 5 August 2019 that extended the application of all provisions of the Constitution of India to Kashmir, the provisions of Article 35A became effectively unconstitutional. It was not withdrawn, it appears, because this provision Article 35A is currently under challenge in the Supreme Court on the ground that, in the first place, Article 35A should have been introduced in the Indian Constitution only through a Constitution Amendment under Article 368 and not through a Presidential Order under Article 370.

Be that as it may, the Presidential Order of 5 August has even amended Article 367, dealing with Interpretations, without following the Amendment Process, but by virtue of power flowing from Article 370.

Potential for problems with 'Special Provisions' for other states

There is a flip side to this episode too. Article 370 and Article 35A stemming out of Article 370 were not unique instances of 'special provisions' in the history of the evolution of the Indian Constitution. For example, Article 371 read with Articles 371A to 371J of the Constitution includes 'special provisions' for 11 states including six states of the North East.

Article 370 and 371 were part of the Constitution at the time of its commencement on 26 January 1950. But Articles 371A, 371B, 371C., etc. were incorporated subsequently. These are briefly explained below:

Article 371A that relates to *Nagaland* was inserted after a 16-point agreement between the Centre and the Naga People's Convention in 1960, which led to the creation of Nagaland in 1963. Parliament cannot legislate in matters of Naga religion or social practices, Naga customary law and procedure, administration civil and criminal justice involving decisions according to Naga customary law, and ownership and transfer of land without concurrence of the State Assembly.

Article 371B that relates to the tribal areas of *Assam* lays down that the President may provide for the constitution and functions of a committee of the Assembly consisting of members elected from the state's tribal areas.

Article 371C that relates to *Manipur* provides that President may provide for the constitution of a committee of elected members from the Hill Areas in the Assembly, and entrust 'special responsibility' to the Governor to ensure its proper functioning.

Article 371D meant for *Andhra Pradesh* and *Telangana* provides that President must ensure 'equitable opportunities and facilities' in 'public employment and education to people from different parts of the state'. He may require the state government to organize 'any class or classes of posts in civil service of, or any class or classes of civil posts under, the State into different local cadres for different parts of the State'. He has similar powers vis-à-vis admission in educational institutions.

Article 371F meant for *Sikkim* provides that the members of the Legislative Assembly of Sikkim shall elect the representative of Sikkim in the House of the People. To protect the rights and interests of various sections of the population of Sikkim, Parliament may provide for the number of seats in the Assembly, which may be filled only by candidates from those sections.

Article 371G meant for *Mizoram* provides that Parliament cannot make laws on 'religious or social practices of the Mizos, Mizo customary law and procedure, administration of civil and criminal justice involving decisions according to Mizo customary law, ownership and transfer of land unless the Assembly … so decides'.

Article 371H meant for *Arunachal Pradesh* provides that the Governor has a special responsibility with regard to law and order, and 'he shall, after consulting the Council of Ministers, exercise his individual judgment as to the action to be taken'.

Article 371J related to *Karnataka* has a provision for a separate development board for the Hyderabad-Karnataka region. There shall be 'equitable allocation of funds for developmental expenditure over the said region' and 'equitable opportunities and facilities' for people of this region in government jobs and education. A proportion of seats in educational institutions and state government jobs in Hyderabad-Karnataka can be reserved for individuals from that region.

After abrogation of the special status that Kashmir was enjoying by virtue of Article 370, apprehensions did arise, about abrogation of special status among the people of the six states of the North East who have also been enjoying 'special status' of different kinds but similar to those of Article 370. Sensing this, the Union Home Minister gave a categorical assurance that Article 371A, 371B, etc., will not be abrogated or even touched since these articles were meant to safeguard the distinctive identities of the North Eastern and other states.

Steps taken on 5 and 6 August in a nutshell

First of all, the Presidential Order C.O. 272 issued on 5 August 2019 used Article 370(1)(d) to apply all provisions of the Indian Constitution other than Articles 1 and 370 to the State of J&K. Articles 1 and 370 were already applicable to the State of J&K by virtue of Article 370(1)(c). It may be recalled that Article 370(1)(d) does allow the President to amend or modify various provisions of the Constitution in relation to J&K, *but with the concurrence of the Government of J&K*. Similar concurrence of the Government of J&K is also needed for the President's exercise of power under Article 370(1)(b)(ii).

In respect of Article 370(3), there is a proviso that there must be the recommendation of the Constituent Assembly of J&K. The J&K Constituent Assembly was dissolved in 1957; thus, there was no Constituent Assembly on 5 August. Further, the State of J&K was under President's Rule from December 2018; therefore obtaining the concurrence of the State Government was an issue during Central Rule (Presidential Rule). The normal course of action in such a case would have been to bring in a Constitutional Amendment that would have required 'two-thirds majority' in the Parliament. But, the Government took an entirely different path.

The Presidential Order C.O. 272 used the power of the President under Article 370(1) to indirectly amend Article

370(3) and Article 370(1) itself, via a third constitutional provision i.e. Article 367. It may be recalled, Article 367 provides various guidelines on interpretation of the Constitution.

The Presidential Order C.O. 272 added a sub-clause to Article 367, replacing the terms 'Constituent Assembly of J&K' to mean 'Legislative Assembly of J&K' and 'Government of J&K' to mean 'Governor of J&K' acting on the aid and advice of the council of ministers. By virtue of the aforesaid amendments of Article 367, the Governor of J&K, who is basically a representative of the Central Government, becomes the Government of J&K. Further, the Legislative Assembly becomes the Constituent Assembly. But, there being no Legislative Assembly as the State is under President's Rule, it fell upon the Parliament to make the recommendations which were to come from the J&K Legislative Assembly in terms of latest amendments through Presidential Order C.O. 272.

Finally, *Article 3* of the Constitution gives Parliament the power to amend the Constitution by a simple majority, to change the boundaries of a state and to form a new state. But this change required that such a Bill be first referred to the concerned State Assembly by the President for ascertaining its views. But there being no Legislative Assembly in J&K, the Second Resolution of the Parliament stated that the President had referred the Jammu & Kashmir Reorganisation Bill, 2019, to the Parliament for its views, since the Parliament is vested with the powers of the State legislature of J&K. On passing of the Second Resolution by Parliament, with effect from 31 October 2019, the State of J&K got bifurcated into two Union Territories.

CHAPTER-V

Debate Starts—Many Issues Raised

Different views of different people

In keeping with the best practices and indeed best traditions of democracy, debate started amongst the Constitution experts, lawyers, academicians, political leaders and common people on the correctness or otherwise of the actions of the Government on 5 and 6 August, and also on various issues arising out those actions.

First, the broad issues are placed below. Thereafter, the views of different people will be explained, based on their written articles and interviews published in print and electronic media after 5 August 2019.

Issues

1. Was it a mistake to insert Article 370 in the Indian Constitution?

2. Was Article 370 just a temporary provision or had it effectively become permanent, since there was no Constituent Assembly in Kashmir to give consent?

3. Can Article 370 be amended by a Presidential Order such as C.O. 272, even indirectly, through amendment of another article of the Constitution? (The example in hand is the

present case where the C.O. 272 has amended Article 367, and used the amended Article 367 to amend Article 370).

4. Can one first use Article 370 to amend Article 367, and thereafter use the amended Article 367 to call the Legislative Assembly the Constituent Assembly?

5. Can the Governor of the state under President's Rule, where there is no Legislative Assembly, be called the State Government?

6. Does the Governor represent the will of the people?

7. How would the conditions in the Instrument of Accession of J&K to India like those in clauses 7 and 8 of the instrument be interpreted, in the context of abrogation of the special status previously provided by Article 370?

8. Is the reorganization of the State of J&K by bifurcating it and converting the parts into Union Territories, without the approval of the State Legislature and the State Government, valid in law?

Views of the People

Issue 1: *Need for Article 370*

On the question about whether it was a mistake to insert Article 370 in the Indian Constitution, **Harish Salve,** former Solicitor General of India and Constitution expert, has said in an interview that it was a mistake to allow Article 370 in the Constitution and a bigger mistake to allow it to fester.

There have been quite a few others supporting Harish Salve's view that Kashmir should have been dealt with like all the other Princely States acceding to India, and that no special treatment should have been meted out to it.

But, there are others who have felt that Article 370 was the need of the hour when it was introduced. Kashmir's case was different from other Princely States—politically, strategically, geopolitically and contractually.

Being located on the north-west tip of India, the State of Kashmir ruled by Maharaja Hari Singh had its borders contiguous to both India and Pakistan; rather its access or exit to the outer world was more through Pakistan across the easily accessible western border. There were not many accessible roads from India in 1947. In terms of the general rule of accession by a Princely State, Kashmir had the option to join either India or Pakistan, both being contiguous to it. Further, Kashmir was a Muslim-majority state. In terms of the general principle of Partition, the Muslim majority Provinces and Princely States were to join Pakistan. **K.M. Chandrasekhar**, former Cabinet Secretary, in his article titled 'Whither Kashmir…?' (dated 10.08.19, in www.pennews.net) has pointed out that Babasaheb Ambedkar also made a reference to the special character of J&K in his resignation speech after quitting the Union Cabinet. The right solution, he said, was to 'partition Kashmir. Give the Hindu and Buddhist part to India and the Muslim part to Pakistan as we did in the case of India. We are really not concerned with the Muslim part of Kashmir'.

Geopolitically and strategically too, Kashmir has always been very important for India. Its northern frontier of Gilgit and Baltistan having borders with Pakistan, North West Frontier Province, Afghanistan and Sinkiang (Xinjiang) Province of China were strategically most important for India. It's a different matter that eventually Gilgit-Baltistan areas were wrongfully and illegally joined to Pakistan with the help of the British Agent in Gilgit, immediately after Kashmir's accession to India. On the other side, Pakistan had been continuously trying through different means to get Kashmir acceded to Pakistan. The framers of the Pakistani Constitution had even kept an article, Article 257 in the Pakistani Constitution that was the equivalent of Article 370 of the Indian Constitution. Article 257 of the Pakistani Constitution had a special provision with special status for Kashmir, 'when Kashmir joins Pakistan'.

Finally, Kashmir acceded to India in terms of an Instrument of Accession which was a sort of a contract between the Governor General of India and Maharaja of Kashmir. Retention of a certain extent of autonomy was a condition laid down in that instrument by virtue of clauses 7 and 8 and certain other words and expressions. Kashmir's accession was not unconditional. In fact, Article 370 was a constitutional recognition of the conditions mentioned in the Maharaja's Instrument of Accession. Thus, Article 370 was an essential facet of our federalism like in the 'compact' or agreement in USA among the 13 British colonies that joined forces to form the original United States.

Considering the facts and circumstances explained above, a conclusion can fairly be drawn that it was imperative for our political leaders Nehru and Patel to have Article 370 and later Article 35A inserted in the Indian Constitution in order to ensure that Kashmir not only joins India, but that its accession to India is made secure too.

It is however a different question whether Article 370 had served its utility and it should have been abrogated much earlier. On this point it may be said emphatically that although Article 370 was not abrogated earlier, it was hollowed out over the years by issuance of Presidential Orders and amendments of Constitutional provisions by using Article 370 itself. In the period from its inception on 26 January till abrogation of its special status on 5 and 6 August 2019, there have been 44 amendments of Article 370. As many as 94 out of 97 entries in the Union List were already made applicable to J&K. Further, 260 out of 395 Articles of the Constitution were already extended and made applicable to J&K. These apart, seven out of 12 Schedules of the Constitution were also already extended to J&K. Besides, over the years the Central Government has used Article 370 to amend a number of provisions of the J&K Constitution, although originally Article 370 had a limited mandate to extend the applicability of the Constitution of India to J&K.

Thus, Article 370 as it was on 4 August 2019, a day before the Government action of August 5, was only a skeleton of what it was on the day of introduction of the Constitution on 26 January 1950; the process of integration of Kashmir into the rest of India had already achieved a lot, even before the recent action of 5 and 6 August 2019.

Issue 2: Article 370—A temporary provision?
On the issue of whether Article 370 was a temporary provision or not, there were a lot of debates.

N. Gopalaswami, Minister in Nehru's government dealing with Kashmir issues, gave an exposition of Article 370 (then introduced as draft 306A) before the Constituent Assembly which has been discussed in Chapter III. While summing up, Gopalaswami explained that Article 370 has been so made that:

> When the Constituent Assembly of the State has met and taken its decision both on the Constitution for the State and on the range of federal jurisdiction over the State, the President may on the recommendation of that Constituent Assembly issue an order that this article 306A (later 307) shall either cease to be operative, or shall be operative only subject to such exceptions and modifications as may be specified by him. *But before he issues any order of that kind the recommendation of the Constituent Assembly will be a condition precedent (emphasis added).*

It may be remembered that the Constituent Assembly for the State of J&K was not in existence when Article 370 was introduced in the Indian Constituent Assembly and Indian Constitution.

Faizan Mustafa, Vice chancellor NALSAR University of Law, is of the view that Article 370 was temporary when it was introduced, because by that time the Constituent Assembly of Kashmir had not been constituted, and it had not met. But when the J&K Constituent Assembly met later, it endorsed Article 370 and said that Kashmir would be governed by it. The Constituent Assembly adopted and ratified a resolution to dissolve itself on 17 November 1956. Thereafter, the Constituent Assembly of Jammu and Kashmir ceased to exist on 26 January 1957. Thus, Article 370 was no longer temporary since the

Constituent Assembly was not there to send its prescribed 'recommendation' to the President.

Soli Sorabjee, former Attorney General, however said that Article 370 was indeed a temporary provision. **Subhash Kashyap**, former Lok Sabha Secretary General supported Soli Sorabjee's views by pointing out that the Constitution-makers clearly, made a distinction between 'temporary' and 'special' provisions; in Article 371, the heading is 'special provisions with regard to Nagaland' whereas in Article 370, the heading says 'temporary provisions with respect to Jammu and Kashmir'.

On the other hand, **Rajeev Dhavan**, senior advocate and constitution lawyer in an interview with Arshu John, the Caravan Asstt. Editor, stated that Article 370 was transitional only to the extent, and until, the Jammu and Kashmir Constitution came into place. That was the temporary part. Otherwise, there was nothing temporary about Article 370. The J&K Constitution framed by an independent Constituent Assembly was a fact—it was a legal fact, a spatial fact and a temporal fact. So, one could not abolish it, as simple as that, said Dhavan.

A.G. Noorani, the Constitutional lawyer and author of many books, cited the exposition of Article 370 by N. Gopalaswami to explain how the temporary status of Article 370 could become final after due consideration by the Constituent Assembly of J&K. He also referred to the views of President Rajendra Prasad on the subject in a note dated 6 September 1952 addressed to Prime Minister Nehru, wherein Rajendra Prasad inter alia, pointed out that the clauses in Article 370 exclude altogether the Parliament of India from having any say regarding the Constitution of Jammu & Kashmir. By referring to the two aforesaid points, Noorani explained how Article 370 became permanent after the Constituent Assembly of J&K was dissolved in 1957.

Justice (Retd) P.B. Sawant, formerly of the Supreme Court, while speaking on the temporary status of Article 370 and the potential danger of clamour for abrogation of Article 370, explained in an article in *The Indian Express* (dated 27 September 2019), that one must not forget the elementary fact that India got the legal right to enter the State of J&K only because of the conditional political pact of accession, and if Article 370 is abrogated unilaterally, the legal right of India to remain in J&K will be jeopardized.

Court rulings

As for the Court rulings, a five-judge bench of the Supreme Court, in the case of Prem Nath Kaul (1959), observed on Article 370(2) that this clause shows that the Constitutional makers attached great importance to the final decision of the Constituent Assembly, and the continuance of the exercise of powers conferred on the Parliament and the President by the relevant temporary provisions of Article 370(1) is '*made conditional on the final approval of the Constituent Assembly of Kashmir*'. The unanimous judgment was authored by five eminent judges—PB Gajendragadkar, S.R. Das, S.K. Das, R.N. Wanchoo and Mohammed Hidaytullah. They unanimously gave the right to take a call on Article 370, exclusively to Kashmir's Constituent Assembly. One may be tempted to infer that in the absence of the Constituent Assembly, it having been dissolved, Article 370 became permanent.

However, in the case of Sampat Prakash (1968), the apex court decided otherwise, and held that Article 370 could be invoked even after the dissolution of the Constituent Assembly. The five-judge Bench said, 'Article 370 has never ceased to be operative'.

But, in 2016, the Supreme Court in the case of *SBI Vs Zaffar Ullah Nehru* observed, inter alia, that J&K has a special status and that Article 370 was not temporary.

Again, in the case of Santosh Kumar (2017) the apex court said that due to historical reasons, the State of Jammu and Kashmir had a special status.

In April, 2018, the Supreme Court said that the word 'temporary' in the head note notwithstanding, Article 370 was not temporary.

In light of the aforementioned discussions that also include contrasting views of lawyers and experts and even different views from the apex court at different times, the best thing to do now is to wait for the apex court to deliver its verdict on the petitions filed recently on various issues, including the present one.

Issues 3 and 4: Can Article 370 be used to amend Article 367 and then the amended Article 367 be used to amend Article 370 itself?

Views in favour of the Government action on these issues:

Harish Salve, in an interview to a TV channel on this issue first made a clarificatory statement that it would be wrong to say that Article 370 was scrapped. It was only that there was a provision in Article 370 itself and by virtue of that provision of

Article 370, a Presidential Order was issued by which the whole of the Indian Constitution was made applicable to matters in Kashmir. He further clarified—in other words, the *Government has used Article 370 to get the exception to the Fundamental Rights that was there in respect of Kashmir, removed by the Presidential Order* and thus its special status was taken away. According to him this action of the *Government was legally correct and it was a means of correcting a mistake.*

Mukul Rohatgi supported Harish Salve's views and maintained that there was no amendment of Article 370, and that there was a Presidential Order in 1954 and there is a new order now in August 2019, which has superseded the 1954 order.

Soli Sorabjee also supported the Government act in stating that under our law, one can change anything in the Constitution that is not its essential feature and if the change does not damage its basic structure. He continued, Article 370 is not an essential feature of the Constitution.

Subhash Kashyap supported the aforementioned views and said that it can be done under Article 370 itself because under Article 370(1), the Central Government can apply any provision of the Constitution to Jammu & Kashmir with the State Government's consent. And now the Government of India is also the Government of Jammu and Kashmir as the state is under President's Rule.

Another view while supporting the Government action is that it cannot be the situation that Article 370 is some kind of royalty, while Article 368 is for the commoners; the will of an extinct Constituent Assembly of J&K cannot be expected to prevail in perpetuity over the will of Parliament.

Views against the Government action on these issues:
Views have also been expressed against the Government decision on the issues of use of Article 370 to amend Article 367, and the use of the said amended Article 367 to amend Article 370 itself. Supreme Court lawyer **Gautam Bhatia** has expressed his views on the subject in his article in Bloomberg Quint (dated 5 August 2019).

Recounting the constitutional provisions, Bhatia explained that Article 370(1) allowed the President to amend or modify various provisions of the Constitution in relation to J&K, but very importantly, with the concurrence of the Government of J&K. Further, Article 370(3) read with its 'proviso' states that Article 370 itself can be amended or repealed by President, provided the Constituent Assembly of J&K recommends so. On 5 August 2019, the State of J&K was under President's Rule, and neither the Constituent Assembly of J&K nor the State Legislature was in existence.

Therefore, the Presidential Order C.O. 272 first of all used the power under Article 370(1) to amend Article 367 which deals with 'interpretation' of the Constitution. By this amendment, the words 'Constituent Assembly' were replaced by the words 'Legislative Assembly of the State' Having done that, the amended Article 367 was used to amend Article 370(3). Based on that, Parliament took over the role of Legislative Assembly and a recommendation was made, in the Statutory Resolution of Parliament to the President, for removal of most of Article 370, leaving behind only Article 370(1).

Bhatia called this step 'very clever' but questions whether it was legal. Bhatia pointed out that Article 370(1)(d) refers to the 'other provisions' of the Constitution, that may be altered by the Presidential Order and not Article 370 itself. One may say that C.O. 272 does not amend Article 370, it amends Article 367 dealing with interpretations. Bhatia however made the point that the contents of those amendments did amend Article 370, and that *one cannot do indirectly what one cannot do directly*— as has been held by Supreme Court in many cases.

Rajeev Dhavan, while opposing the Government action, pointed out that the Presidential Order sought to supersede the J&K Constitution. However, the same order mentions the expressions 'Constituent Assembly of the State' and 'Legislative Assembly of the State'. Obviously the Legislative Assembly is under the State of Jammu and Kashmir Constitution. Thus, the same very order recognized the Constitution of Jammu & Kashmir which it sought to supersede. 'How could it be done?' asked Rajeev Dhavan.

On the argument that the Presidential Order amended Article 367, and that technically it has not amended Article 370, Dhavan pointed out that all Article 367 was saying was how would one interpret the Constitution. *It's an interpretation provision and it did not give substantive powers.* On the Government action of adding a provision to Article 367 to change the interpretation of Article 370, Dhavan said what Gautam Bhatia also had said—one cannot do indirectly what one cannot do directly.

Justice P.B. Sawant, while opposing the Government action in the context of the issues under discussion, in an article published in *The Indian Express* (dated 27 September 19) pointed out that Article 370(3) made it abundantly clear that the provisions of the said Article will not cease to be operative or modified *without the previous recommendation of the Constituent Assembly of the J&K state.* The process of amendment of Article 370 is special to the said Article, and hence it prevails over Article 368, which is the general power of amendment of the Constitution. Thus, Sawant stated that in this case the procedure laid down in Article 370 was not followed, and therefore Article 370 remained in our Constitution intact without any harm to it.

A.G. Noorani expressed his views in an article (dated 13 August 2019) published in The Wire. He stated, inter alia, that the Government's decision to scrap the J&K Constitution is not permissible under Article 370. Article 370 limits the President's power to apply to the State of J&K only for certain items agreed in terms of the Instrument of Accession. But, if the Presidential Order seeks to go beyond those, the concurrence of the Assembly of J&K would be necessary.

The Constituent Assembly of J&K met in the later part of 1956, adopted the J&K State's Constitution and then dissolved the Constituent Assembly with effect from 26 January 1957. So, Noorani explained that these developments ended the President's powers under Article 370, to add more legislative powers to the Centre in respect of J&K or extend to the State of J&K any other provisions of the Constitution of India. Noorani also pointed out that Article 370 referred to the J&K Constituent Assembly twice, thus *recognizing its right to have its own Constitution and that right could not be nullified by an executive order by the President* at the instance of the Central Government.

He further stated that Article 1 of India's Constitution establishing a 'Union of States' applies to J&K by virtue of Article 370(1)(c). He also said that in 1993 the Home Minister S.B. Chavan pointed out that Article 370 was *the only link* India had with Kashmir. Later in June 1996, Narasimha Rao said, 'Abrogation of this Article is just not possible, unless you want to part with the state' (Noorani, The Wire, 13 Aug. 2019).

On clause 2(d) of the Presidential Order, Noorani expressed shock that it amended Article 370(3) to replace the words 'Constituent Assembly of the State' with the words 'Legislative Assembly of the State'. He pointed out that a Constituent Assembly was a body wielding constituent powers as a sovereign body. It itself establishes a Legislative Assembly with limited powers it defines. The J&K Constituent Assembly ceased to exist on 26 January 1957. The Legislative Assembly it created in J&K's Constitution still survives by virtue of Article 46. 'How can one now endow it with constituent power to accord its concurrence to the Centre to destroy the State's autonomy?' asked Noorani. Finally, Noorani cautioned as follows:

> Remember, Article 370 is no mere provision enacted by the Constituent Assembly of India. It gives effect to a solemn compact negotiated over five long months between the Government of India and the Government of Jammu and Kashmir. History will never forgive those who wrecked it calculatedly since May, 1954 and then demolished it on August 5, 2019 (Noorani, The Wire, 13 Aug. 2019).

Faizan Mustafa, Vice Chancellor, NALSAR University of Law has given his reasons for not supporting the Government actions of 5 and 6 August in an article written in www.theindiaforum.in. Mustafa explained that Article 370 is nothing but a Constitutional recognition of the conditions mentioned in the Instrument of Accession, and it reflects the contractual rights and obligations of the two parties. He further elaborated that Article 370 is an essential facet of our federalism, and it governs the Centre's relationship with Jammu & Kashmir.

Mustafa further stated that Article 370(3) could certainly be deleted by a Presidential Order; but due to the proviso given in this clause, such an order has to be preceded by the recommendation of the Constituent Assembly of J&K. However, since the Constituent Assembly was dissolved, one view is that Article 370(3) cannot be deleted and it has acquired a permanent status. The other view is that Article 370(3) could probably be deleted with the concurrence of the State Legislative Assembly, which represents the will of the people through the elected representatives.

He then added that even while the core of Article 370 has been eroded, it did have huge sentimental value for the people of Jammu & Kashmir who would view the abrogation with the great deal of unhappiness. He also reminded that it would be a violation of commitments given at the time of accession of Jammu & Kashmir. He further said that *Article 370 is certainly not an issue of integration, and that it is an issue of granting autonomy or federalism.* Those who advocate its deletion are more concerned with uniformity rather than integration. Uniformity and integration are not the one and the same.

Preservation of diversity and granting autonomy indeed lead to integration, Mustafa concluded.

While opposing the Government action, **Shadan Farasat**, Senior Advocate, stated that Article 367 can be amended by a Presidential Order insofar as it applied to the State of Jammu & Kashmir. But, the Government cannot try to amend Article 370 by using Article 367. Article 370 cannot be amended by a Presidential Order because of Article 370(1)(c). Farasat pointed out that the *application of Article 370 and Article 1 is not through a Presidential Order, but through Article 370 itself*. It is important to note that Article 370(1)(d) goes on to say that aside from Article 1 and Article 370, one can apply it through a presidential Order with appropriate amendments, etc.

Farasat concluded by saying that effectively, the Government was amending Article 370 by amending Article 367, which was not permissible. Otherwise, what was the meaning of Article 370, he asked. He reiterated that *amending Article 370 through a Presidential Order was beyond the terms of Article 370 itself*.

P. Chidambaram, senior lawyer and former Home Minister, in an article in *The Indian Express* (dated 11 August 2019), while referring to the Government action where 'Article 370 was replaced by invoking clause (1) of Article 370 and amending clause(3) of Article 370', stated that 'whether it was a fatal legal error or an over-clever legal stratagem, only time and the courts can tell. Mortals like us can only describe it as a constitutional maneuver worthy of the well-known contortionist Sofie Dossi. The new Article 370 with just one clause is no longer a special provision, it simply applies the whole of the Constitution to J&K'.

Chidambaram also stated that the repeal of Article 370 will be regarded as a breach of a constitutional guarantee as well as a breach of promise, made by Jawaharlal Nehru, Sardar Vallabhbhai Patel (assisted by N. Gopalaswami Ayyangar and V.P. Menon), Babasaheb Ambedkar and the other makers of the Constitution. He added that the people will also regard the actions as repudiation of A.B. Vajpayee's famous statement that a solution to the Kashmir issue will be found within '*Insaniyat, Jamhooriyat and Kashmiriyat*' (humanity, democracy and the composite culture of Kashmir).

While opposing Government action, a report from **Reuters** (dated 5 August 2019) stated that going by the views of Constitutional experts and Supreme Court lawyers, India's move 'to strip Kashmir of special rights' is likely to face legal challenges. Some of the experts questioned the legality of the route used to make the change. The report said that according to the lawyers and constitution experts, the following problematic issues are likely to be taken up in the courts:

a. Absence of concurrence or recommendation from the Constituent Assembly since it was dissolved in 1957;
b. Treatment of 'Legislative Assembly' as 'Constituent Assembly';
c. Treatment of 'Parliament' as 'Legislative Assembly', where Legislative Assembly is not there due to President's Rule;
d. Treatment of 'Governor' as the State Government;

Issue 5: Can the Governor of the State be called the State Government?

This issue arises particularly in a case where the state is under President's Rule, and there is no Legislative Assembly. **Gautam Bhatia** has explained the issue lucidly in his previously mentioned article in Bloomberg Quint.

In respect of the much discussed actions taken on August 5 and 6, the Presidential Order C.O. 272 says that the concurrence of the Government of the State of J&K has been taken. But the State of J&K was already under President's Rule. Therefore, the concurrence mentioned in the C.O. 272 was that of the Governor of the State. Bhatia has pointed out two serious problems arising out of the proposition that the Governor is the State Government and his consent has to be treated as the consent of the State Government.

The first problem is that the Governor is a representative of the Central Government, just as the President is. In effect, therefore, Presidential Order 272 amounts to the Central Government taking its own consent through the Governor to amend the Constitution. Secondly, which is a more important issue, President's Rule is temporary and is meant to be a stand-in until the elected government is restored. Consequently, a decision of a permanent character, such as the present one of changing the entire status of the State, taken without the elected legislative assembly, but by the Governor, is inherently problematic. Bhatia pointed out that formally these may be within the bounds of legality; but, as Supreme Court held in the case of D.C. Wadhwa, on the question of re-promulgation of ordinances, formal legality can none the less, in effect, amount to a fraud on the Constitution. Bhatia reiterated that *using the Governor to sign off on a Presidential order that fundamentally alters the constitutional character of a federal unit appears to be straying dangerously close to the constitutional fraud line.*

A.G. Noorani stated on the present issue that the Presidential Order is made avowedly with the concurrence of the Government of J&K, but no such government had existed there for over a year, evidently 'to facilitate this Constitutional skullduggery' through the Governor. Noorani then pointed out that Article 370 itself defined 'the government of the state' in the 'Explanation', and in terms of that Explanation, *the Governor could not act under Article 370 singly as 'the government of the state'.* He emphasized that the object of the provision was to buttress the state's autonomy. So the Center's appointee could not give his concurrence to the Centre.

Noorani concluded on this particular issue by stating that the order under Article 370 was made with the concurrence of the Centre's appointee, the Governor on the pretext that he was the State Government, but after 1951, when the J&K Constituent Assembly was convened, the State Government had lost its interim power to accord consent. It now belonged to the Constituent Assembly but the Constituent Assembly was dissolved in 1957. Only the State Legislative Assembly remained. By the actions of August 2019, the State Legislative Assembly was converted to Constituent Assembly with retrospective effect, and the Governor of the State of J&K was turned into the Government of J&K State. For the reasons explained in foregoing paragraphs, Noorani maintained that the *Governor, the Centre's appointee, could not act as the State Government and grant ascent to the Centre.*

Issue 6: Does the Governor represent the 'Will of the People'? When asked in an *Outlook* interview whether the Governor represents the will of the people, **Soli Sorabjee** maintained that 'it is a grey area' (19 August 2019).

Subhash Kashyap stated that the Governor is not elected by the people but appointed by the President, who is elected by people's representatives in both houses of Parliament and all State Legislative Assemblies. Thus, he represents the people of India, including the people of Jammu & Kashmir.

Faizan Mustafa emphatically said 'no'. He pointed out that the Governor represents the will of the Central Government, he is a nominee of the Centre. The Governors of the States in India have proved to be agents of the Centre in the State. They have not shown their commitment to the Constitution; their commitment has been to the party in power at the Centre. So, Mustafa concluded that *they cannot be called representatives of the people since they are nominated and not elected by the people.*

Colin Gonsalves, Supreme Court Advocate, while supporting the views of Faizan Mustafa said emphatically that Governor does not represent the 'will of the people'. He said that if one looks at the history of the Instrument of Accession, it was the Constituent Assembly and the State Assembly whose concurrence would have to be taken and certainly not the Governor. The reason is that the *Sadar-i-Riyasat was an elected member and the Governor is not.*

Harish Salve and **Mukul Rohatgi** supported the Government action basically on the ground that the *President has passed the Presidential Order in terms of the authority vested in him, including the authority to amend Article 367.*

Issue 7: How would the conditions in the Instrument of Accession of J&K be interpreted in the context of abrogation of the special status previously provided by Article 370?

Faizan Mustafa, in an article on Article 370 written in www. theindiaforum.in expressed the following views on the issue.

Explaining the history of Article 370, Mustafa stated that Article 370 reflects the contractual rights and obligations of two parties i.e. the ruler of Kashmir and Government of India. The *conditions mentioned in the Instrument of Accession have got Constitutional recognition in Article 370, and thus Article 370 governs the Centre's relationship with Jammu & Kashmir.*

Mustafa cited Section 6(a) of the 1947 Act in stating that *the act of joining one of the two countries was to be through an Instrument of Accession. Thus, the Instrument of Accession was supposed to regulate and govern the distribution of powers between the Central Government and the concerned Princely State.*

Mustafa therefore stated that technically speaking, the Instrument of Accession was like a treaty between two sovereign countries which had decided to work together. Further he explained that the maxim under the international law which governs contracts or treaties between states is *Pacta sunt servanda* i.e. promises between states must be honoured. It there is a breach of contract, the general rule is that parties involved are to be restored to the original position, i.e. the pre-agreement status.

Thereafter, Mustafa cautioned that in any talk of abrogation of Article 370, this aspect of international law must be kept in mind because *if due to the breach of any condition of the Instrument of Accession, the princely state of Kashmir gets its pre-accession status, it will obviously not be in India's interest.* He also reminded that the Schedule appended to the Instrument of Accession gave the Indian Parliament power to legislate for Jammu & Kashmir on only defence, external affairs and communications. Further, *through clauses 5, and 7 in the Instrument of Accession, the Maharaja of Kashmir ensured a certain amount of sovereignty for Jammu & Kashmir.* Indeed, Article 370 was the tunnel through which the Constitution of India was applied in Kashmir.

Justice (Retd) P.B. Sawant stated on this issue,

> Those who clamour for the abrogation of Article 370 unilaterally by this government, forget the elementary fact that this country got legal right to enter the state only because of the conditional political pact of accession. *If the Article is abrogated unilaterally, assuming the action is valid, the legal right of this country to remain in J&K will be jeopardized* (*Indian Express,* 27 Sept. 2019).

This is another contentious issue for resolution of which one will have to wait for the apex court judgment.

Issue 8: Is the reorganization of the State of J&K by bifurcating it and converting the two parts into Union

Territories, without the approval of State Legislature and the State Government, valid in law?

Soli Sorabjee's reply, when asked by *India Today* on 6 August 2019, was, 'Kashmir is an integral part of India. I don't see anything unconstitutional in the Bill for reorganization of the State. But, the court will have to decide whether the consent of the J&K Governor was enough. It's a grey area.' Later, in an interview given to the magazine *Outlook,* **Soli Sorabjee** said that there is a need for more consultation with the people. 'Now, though, it is a fact of history' (19 August 2019).

Subhash Kashyap, answered *Outlook,* on the aforesaid question, in the affirmative as well as negative: Yes, because the Constitution provided for the consent of the State Government, and no, because there was no State Government at the time of Presidential Order, the State of J&K being under President's Rule. Kashyap clarified that since J&K was under President's Rule, the Government of India was also the government of the State, and Parliament of India was the State Legislature. Kashyap also argued that the Government of India was an elected government, and so it cannot be said that there was no elected government.

Colin Gonsalves, Supreme Court Advocate, said that the crux of the matter was whether the State reorganization can take place on the basis of a Presidential notification, or whether it needs Parliament's consent. According to Gonsalves, under Article 370 (3), it cannot be done by a Presidential notification; it must be done by Parliament itself.

Shahdan Farasat said in the *Outlook* interview that there is no case in the history of the Indian Union where a new state has been formed by treating Parliament as a State Legislature during President's Rule. Farasat pointed out that the Government was treating Parliament as the State Legislature for the purpose of reference. That cannot be done. It's totally an abuse of the provisions of the Constitution. He further explained that under Article 3, one has to take the view of the State Legislature. But, there was no legislature in J&K since the inception of President's Rule. Whenever there is Presidential Rule, if some bills have to be passed, Parliament exercises that power under proclamation of Article 356. So, Parliament functions as a State Legislature. But surely, 'when the Proviso of Article 3 is itself a check on the Parliament, then how can one treat that also as Parliament'? Further, the text of Article 3 only permits reducing the territory of a State by converting part of a State into another state(s) Union Territory. However, it does not envisage reduction of the entire territory of a state into Union Territories. *India is a Union of States as per Article 1 and it will be reduced to a 'Union of Union Territories if this is allowed.'*

Faizan Mustafa said in the *Outlook* interview that under Article 3, a bill to change the boundaries or name of the State or, bifurcation of the state should be first referred by the President to the concerned legislative assembly for ascertaining its views. Here it could not be done due to dissolution of Jammu & Kashmir Assembly. Under President's Rule, powers of the Assembly are exercised by Parliament. Mustafa pointed out that in this case, Parliament exercised this power and a fresh Presidential Order was issued on 6 August, after referring to the Resolution of the Parliament. He concluded by saying that this might have been in compliance with the text of the Constitution, but was certainly contrary to its spirit.

Harish Salve, stated in a T.V. interview in total support of the Government action that *reorganizations of states involves a political process and it is constitutional too. In this case, Parliament, acting as an Assembly proposed and the Government has done it.* He asserted that there was nothing unconstitutional about it.

P. Chidambaram, however differed. In his article written in *The Indian Express* (dated 11 August 2019), he gave his opinion on obtaining the views of the Parliament on the proposal to dismember the State of J&K and create two Union Territories. He stated that the right to express views had been vested in the State Constituent Assembly that had drafted the J&K Constitution. But in one stroke, the State Constituent Assembly became the State Legislative Assembly of J&K, and then became Parliament. Chidambaram explained, thus Parliament passed the Resolution, after obtaining the views of Parliament. On reorganizing the State of J&K, Chidambaram said that the Jammu & Kashmir (Reorganisation) Bill, 2019, pretended to follow past precedents that had created two states out of one, except that the Bill created two Union Territories out of one state. He also cautioned that this has set a bad precedent. If this precedent is followed, in future the routine will be to ask the State Assembly to 'express its views' or impose President's Rule and dissolve the Assembly. He also stated that *more important issues are not the legal questions but the political questions*—the Government did not consult the Legislative Assembly of J&K before the Assembly was dissolved, or the mainstream political parties or the people through the interlocutors, etc.

Jamyang Tsering, MP from Ladakh, supported bifurcation and separate territorial identity of Ladakh. He stated that right since 1948, the President of the Ladakh Buddhist Association had been requesting for either bringing Ladakh directly under the Central administration or for making it a part of East Punjab. But the Central Government did not listen to their interest and hence Ladakh fell far behind in development work. He also hoped that now Ladakh's future would be bright.

Karan Singh, the son of Maharaja Hari Singh, the last ruler of Kashmir and a veteran political leader, welcomed the Government's decision to make Ladakh a Union Territory, separated from Jammu & Kashmir, thus signaling that he was in favour of bifurcation of J&K. He even said that in 1965 when he was still *Sadar-i-Riyasat* of J&K, he had publicly proposed reorganization of the State of J&K. *He also hoped that the Hill Councils of Leh and Kargil would continue to function, so that in the absence of the Legislature, the grass roots opinion of the people of Ladakh are duly represented.*

K.M. Chandrasekhar, in his previously mentioned article (in www.pennnews.net) has also stated that making Ladakh a Union Territory is something the people of Leh, primarily Buddhist, have been demanding for years. On the other hand, the people of Kargil, predominantly Shia Muslims would be very unhappy. Chandrasekhar is however happy that the breakup of J&K remained with a bifurcation rather than a trifurcation, proposed on an earlier occasion in 2000, on religious lines—Kashmir Valley with predominately Muslims, Jammu with predominantly Hindus and Ladakh with predominantly

Buddhists. Chandrasekhar pointed out that a bifurcation leaves the Hindus and Muslims together in J&K and Buddhists and Shia Muslims together in Ladakh.

Miscellaneous issues arising out of Government actions of 5 and 6 August 2019

Rajmohan Gandhi, Columnist, while opposing the Government in an article written in *The Indian Express* (dated 19 August 2019) cautioned the Government about the *danger of not taking people's consent*. Emphasizing that all healthy human involvements require the other person's consent, Gandhi stated that even if the actions of August 2019 lead to Kashmir's overall development, prosperity, harmony etc., *a people whose consent was never taken will despise their rulers*. He also stated that any message about Kashmir that India wishes to send to China or Pakistan would be stronger if Kashmiris endorse it. Further, if there is any road towards better relations between Kashmiris and the rest of India, that road must contain a few Indians, official and private, who nurse a desire to win Kashmiri minds. Gandhi finally lamented that no one had also thought of seeking the consent of the peaks, waters and trees of Kashmir, before destroying the nature, environment and ecology of Kashmir by taking away its special status and facilitating easy access to Kashmir's natural resources.

Prof. Ashutosh Varshney, while opposing the Government action, explained in an article in *The Indian Express* (dated 17 August 2019) that the change in Jammu & Kashmir's constitutional status was democratic only in one sense—it had parliamentary majority, and that democracy was much more than that. According to him, democracy has at least four meanings.

First of all, *democracy is a system of electoral power*. Having received a massive mandate, removal of Article 370 benefits for Kashmir is consistent with the first meaning of democracy—namely, electoral majorities as a cornerstone of democratic power.

The second idea of *democracy*, according to Varshney *is that it is also a system of minority protection*. He explained that the minority protection principle of democracy means that even with 229 million overwhelmingly Hindu votes, the winning party should not impose its will on seven million Kashmiris. The agreements made to protect minority rights i.e. *Articles 370 and 35A would have to be respected, unless the minority itself agreed to their termination.*

The third meaning of *democracy is that it is a constitutionally governed system*. Varshney clarified that the elections establish who will rule, but the rulers so elected are also constitutionally bound. Here, *there are three key questions*. First, can routine legislative action scrap an article of the Constitution? Or, was a mandatory constitutional amendment required? Second, can the Governor's approval be taken as the State's consent for change?

According to Varshney, the Governor could not be called a substitute for the state's elected political representative. Third, can India's Parliament, without a Constitutional Amendment, turn a state with full federal rights into a Union Territory, which has reduced rights and whose law and order are centrally governed and not by the state?

After explaining the three key questions relating to the third meaning of democracy, Varshney presented the *fourth meaning of democracy which according to him is a system of political ethics*. In a democracy, those vitally affected by a decision are given a chance to speak, even if they are likely or destined to lose. Varshney said that the Kashmir Valley was vitally affected by this constitutional change, but the people were silenced through various means.

Varshney concluded by saying that *only in one democratic sense—democracy as a system of electoral power could the decision to change Kashmir's statutes be called potentially legitimate*. In all other democratic senses, it was a failure. Summing up, he said that *it was electorally enabled brute majoritarianism*.

Haseeb A. Drabu, former Finance Minister of the State of J&K in a government run jointly by BJP and PDP, a Kashmiri political party, wrote in *The Indian Express* (dated 12 September 2019) *about the consequences of abrogation and serious implications of* reorganization of the State of J&K on the definition of the 'territory' of J&K.

First of all, Drabu invited the attention to the Constitution of India, Clause 3 of Article 1, which states that the territory of India shall comprise the territories of the states. The First Schedule lists out all the states in the Union and defines their individual territorial limits. In the process, it defines the territory of India. There is no other definition of the territory of India as a whole in the Constitution save as a sum of its parts. As the 15th state in the Union, the territorial boundaries of J&K are defined in the First Schedule as, 'The territory which immediately before the commencement of this Constitution was comprised in the *Indian* State of Jammu and Kashmir' *(emphasis added)*. Drabu pointed out that unlike all other states whose boundaries are precisely defined, this territorial definition of Jammu and Kashmir is not only ambiguous but also contentious.

Drabu pointed out that, the use of the word 'Indian' in the term 'Indian State of Jammu & Kashmir' is problematic, particularly because all other states listed in the First Schedule of the Constitution do not have the prefix 'Indian' while describing the Territories.

Drabu further explained that there are two parts to this definition: First, the phrase 'immediately before the commencement of this Constitution'. Which precise date does this refer to? And second, what does the term 'Indian State of Jammu and Kashmir' mean? This is the only place in the Constitution of India, where the prefix 'Indian' has been added to the 'state of Jammu and Kashmir' or for that matter to any other state. In all other references to it in the Constitution, the word used is 'State of Jammu and Kashmir'. Nowhere does the Constitution of India define what comprises the 'Indian State of Jammu and Kashmir'. Even historically, Maharaja Hari Singh signed the Instrument of Accession with India on 26 October 1947 for his entire state; and not the Indian State of Jammu and Kashmir'. So where did the term emanate from and what does it signify? More importantly, what does it connote in terms of its physical boundaries?

Drabu gave an answer to these questions when he explained that the Constituent Assembly of India used this term in the context of the Government of India's reference to the UN on its territorial dispute with Pakistan over Kashmir in January

1948. The Constituent Assembly chose not to pre-empt the UN settlement by including the entire state of Jammu and Kashmir as a part of India. The UN had mediated the cessation of hostilities in 1949 and drew a ceasefire line that left 35 per cent of the total area under control of Pakistan. This became the de facto border, the Line of Control with Pakistan Occupied Kashmir, under the Simla Agreement in 1972.

Drabu continued saying that the Constituent Assembly debates and the correspondence between the main dramatis personae indeed discussed the eventuality of the state deciding to join Pakistan, post the promised plebiscite and its implication on the Constitution of India. As such, the *territory mentioned in the First Schedule of the Constitution means the territory of Jammu and Kashmir under the control of India.* Hence, also, the qualification 'Indian', said Drabu.

The phrase 'immediately before the commencement of this Constitution' can either mean when the Constituent Assembly of India formally adopted the Constitution, that is, 26 November 1949. Or it can be 26 January 1950 when it was promulgated. Taking either date, more than one-third of the state, was under the 'illegal' occupation of Pakistan. Did the Constitution of India, then, forego its claim on Pakistan Occupied Kashmir? The answer is no', said Drabu emphatically.

Drabu then proceeded to explain why the territory of India was ambiguously defined in the Constitution of India, and how this issue had been settled in the Constitution of the State of Jammu and Kashmir, *and also how the consequence of rendering the Constitution of J&K infructuous could damage India's interest on the issue of Pakistan Occupied Kashmir.*

Drabu clarified that the territory of J&K has been ambiguously defined in the Constitution of India because the Constituent Assembly of India did the politically correct thing of leaving it to the Constituent Assembly of Jammu and Kashmir to discuss, deliberate and define it. The territory of Jammu and Kashmir is defined comprehensively in the now rescinded Constitution of Jammu and Kashmir. The Constitution of Jammu and Kashmir, Part II, para 4, states that '*The territory of the State shall comprise all the territories which on the fifteenth day of August, 1947, were under the sovereignty or suzerainty of the Ruler of the State*'. By this definition, the territory of the state of Jammu and Kashmir includes *not only the existing state but also the areas occupied by Pakistan* (what they call Azad Jammu and Kashmir and Gilgit-Baltistan) and those areas which were ceded to China in 1963 (Shaksgam tract, now a part of the Xinjiang Uygur autonomous region).

Drabu continued, this, read with Part II, para (3) of the Constitution of Jammu and Kashmir, which states, 'The State of Jammu and Kashmir is and shall be an integral part of the Union of India' amplifies the definition of the 'Indian state of Jammu and Kashmir' mentioned in the Constitution of India. The point is that *it was the Constitution of Jammu and Kashmir and not the Constitution of India which made the full territory of Jammu and Kashmir an integral part of the Union of India*. In other words, the Constitution of India was dependent on the Constitution of Jammu and Kashmir in this regard, claimed Drabu.

To substantiate the point he made, he stated that the Constitution of Jammu and Kashmir even provided 25 seats in the state legislature for the elected representatives of the 'occupied' areas. It was stipulated, under Section 48 (I) of the Constitution of Jammu and Kashmir, that these seats would remain vacant (and reserved) and would not be taken into account for reckoning the total membership of the assembly, till these areas of the state remain under occupation. Significantly, the J&K State Reorganisation Act 2019, had reduced the number of these vacant seats to 24. *Is this formalising the Aksai Chin ceding?* wondered Drabu.

Drabu further pointed out that the significance of the territorial definition goes beyond the boundaries of J&K. It is on the basis of this definition of the territory of J&K in the Constitution of Jammu and Kashmir that the territorial limits of India got axiomatically defined. Now, with the Constitution (Application to Jammu and Kashmir) Order 2019, the *Constitution of Jammu & Kashmir has been rendered infructuous. Along with that goes away the constitutionally defined territorial limits of J&K.* Drabu wondered, did it mean that the Government of India has, constitutionally speaking, given up its claims on Pakistan Occupied Kashmir and also the territories that Pakistan illegally ceded to China?

In the final paragraph, Drabu has explained the reasons why the Supreme Court could strike down the Constitution Order 2019; given the fact that the territory of India is an aggregation of the territories of the states, the Constitution Order 2019 has effectively changed the territorial boundary of India. While the Constitution explicitly provides for expansion, of 'such other territories as may be acquired', *there is no provision for Parliament to reduce the territory of India.* Yet, that is precisely what the Constitution Order 2019 has done. This in itself is a sufficient ground for it to be struck down by the Supreme Court, Drabu concluded.

Gopal Sankaranarayanan, Supreme Court Advocate, in an article in *The Indian Express* (dated 4 September 2019) pointed out that the foundation of the entire exercise of issuance of Presidential Orders on 5 and 6 August was imposition of President's Rule in the State of Jammu & Kashmir in December 2018 and that the Central Government had not renewed the President's Rule in J&K in time, in accordance with Article 356 of the Constitution, and its consequences were grave.

He explained that Article 356 of the Constitution allows the President to impose his rule on a state where he is satisfied that governance is not in accordance with the Constitution. The proclamation he/she issues in this regard can also provide for the vesting of the powers of government in the President, that of the legislature in Parliament and most significantly, the suspension of the provisions of the Constitution that would apply to a body or authority in the state. He pointed out that in our Westminster form of government, this essentially means the central government can abuse Article 356 to impose its will on states where inconvenient opposition parties are in power. However, anticipating this possible misuse, the Constituent Assembly provided two principal safeguards in Article 356: First, that every proclamation would be valid for only two months; and second, if resolutions approving the proclamation were passed by both Houses of Parliament, then it would be valid for six months, which could be extended up to a maximum period of three years with parliamentary resolutions on each occasion. The exact words of Article 356(4) are: 'A Proclamation so approved shall, unless revoked, cease to operate on the expiration of a period of six months from the date of issue of the Proclamation.'

Sankaranarayanan pointed out that as far as Jammu and Kashmir is concerned, the President first issued his Proclamation on 19 December 2018, vesting the powers of the government with himself and those of the legislature with Parliament. This was followed on 3 January 2019 by the approval of the Houses of Parliament. Notably, this approval gave the Proclamation a life of *six months with effect from 19 December 2018*. Therefore, if it were not extended before 18 June, the *Proclamation in the solemn words of the Constitution, would 'cease to operate'*.

In 1994, a nine-judge bench of the Supreme Court in the *S.R. Bommai case had observed that the necessary consequence of such a lapse of the Proclamation would be that the status quo ante revives* and the Legislative Assembly which may have been kept in suspended animation also springs back to life. According to Sankaranarayanan the only option was a fresh Proclamation to be issued by the President on the same terms as the earlier one. *Neither the notifications by the President on 5 and 6 August under Article 370, nor the exercise by Parliament to reorganise the state as two Union Territories were carried out with the approval of the J&K state legislature.* In fact, both the top nation's executive of Centre and the legislature (Parliament) proceeded as if the legislature did not exist, *singularly on the understanding that the Proclamation was still in force.* Sankaranarayanan concluded that the consequence appears to be grave—'gubernatorial privilege has been peculated and the creation of new territories to be directly governed by the Centre has undermined the federal canon. India and its government have had to endure obloquy, both from within and without'.

Salil Tripathi, an independent writer based in London, wrote opposing the Government's action, in the Opinion Column of *Live Mint* on 7 August, a piece titled 'Some difficult questions on the state of affairs in Kashmir'. He started by stating that after India sought the United Nations' intervention, two outcomes were expected—Pakistani infiltrators would go back and India would hold a plebiscite. Neither happened. India did hold state and national elections in which Kashmiris participated but sometimes boycotted. India has since argued that Kashmiri participation in these elections shows their acceptance of the accession. He further stated that the move on Article 370 was risky, constitutionally questionable and relied on legal sophistry: The 'special status' was not revoked, but enfeebled and the state was broken up. In doing this, the government has not consulted people in J&K—which is under President's rule.

While stating that legal challenges of the J&K decisions are certain, Tripathi wondered, would the courts, wash their hands of the issue, saying this is a political matter for politicians to decide? He continued saying that beyond the legal cleverness used and the assault on federalism, there is a profoundly moral question. When the Aadhaar bill was passed as a money bill, Justice Dhananjay Chandrachud, in his dissenting opinion, had called it 'a fraud' on the Constitution. He pointed out that it is a judicial axiom that a state should not do indirectly what it cannot do directly.

Tripathi raised several other questions. Is democracy to be observed in form or also in substance? Is Parliament a place where decisions are only to be announced and approved, giving minimal preparation time for the Opposition even to absorb the provisions, or is it meant to be a discursive body? And, more importantly, Tripathi wondered whether a state's promise that it would honour the spirit of a Treaty of Accession carry any meaning? Substantive changes required the consent of the governed, but instead, the Centre's representative, the Governor, has become the representative of the State and its people. He concluded by saying that the contracts between the citizens and their State have been discarded and the spirit of the Constitution challenged.

Afterword

It is evident that there are many issues that are controversial, inasmuch as opposing views have been expressed by the columnists, lawyers and constitutional experts. To start with eight such basic issues were identified and the experts have given their views on each of the said eight issues. Besides these eight specific issues, the experts have raised certain other important issues related to the Government's actions in August 2019. All these issues are listed below for the convenience of readers:

1. Was it a mistake to insert Article 370 in the Indian Constitution?
2. Was Article 370 just a temporary provision? Or, has it effectively become permanent because of the absence of the Constituent Assembly of J&K to give its consent?
3. Can Article 370 be amended by a Presidential Order indirectly, through amendment of another article of the Constitution?
4. Can Article 370 be used first to amend Article 367, and then the amended Article 367 be used to call the Legislative Assembly of J&K as the Constituent Assembly?
5. Where there is no Legislative Assembly, can the Governor of the State under President's Rule be called the State Government?

6. Does the Governor of the State represent the will of the people of that state?

7. How would the conditions in the Instrument of Accession of J&K be interpreted in the context of abrogation of special status previously provided by Article 370?

8. Is this reorganization of the State of J&K by the Central Government without the approval of State Legislature and State Government valid in Law?

Subsidiary General Issues

1. In a healthy democracy isn't it supreme to have the consent of people?

2. Is it not necessary for healthy sustenance of democracy to comply with four basic parameters as follows –that it is:

    a) a system of electoral majorities ;
    b) also a system of minority protection;
    c) a constitutionally governed system; and,
    d) a system of political ethics.

3. Is it not a fact that it was the Constitution of Jammu & Kashmir and not the Constitution of India which made the full territory of J&K, including POK, Gilgit-Baltistan and Aksai Chin an integral part of the Union of India?

4. In that sense, hasn't the reduction in the territory of India (by virtue of abrogation of the Constitution of the State of J&K) done away with the constitutionally defined bigger territorial area of J&K and thus has been an act of violation of the Constitution of India?

5. The proclamation of the Presidential Order having been valid for six months from 19 December 2018, did the proclamation cease to operate after 18 June 2019 and if so, did not the State Legislature get revived immediately after 18 June, thus bringing in the requirement of approval by the J&K Legislature before the Presidential Orders dated 5 and 6 August 2019?

6. Will the actions of the Government on 5 and 6 August 2019 be covered by the judicial axiom that a *state should not do indirectly what it cannot do directly*?

7. Is democracy to be observed only in form or also in substance; is Parliament a place where decisions are only to be announced and approved, giving minimal preparation time for all Members of Parliament including those from the Opposition?

8. Are the apprehensions in the minds of people from the States of Nagaland, Arunachal Pradesh, Assam, etc., of the North East, regarding the possibility of future abrogation of 'special status' similar to Article 370 given to them, correct?

As the debate rages on about these issues, as expected, petitions started getting filed in the Supreme Court by people from various walks of life. The petitioners included politicians, activists and media personnel. One of the first filed petitions was by *Mohammed Akbar Lone, former Speaker of the J&K Assembly and Justice (Retd) Hasnain Masoodi, former Judge of the J&K High Court,* both Lok Sabha members belonging to the National Conference (NC).

While challenging the Centre's decisions to scrap the provisions of Article 370 and to divide the State of J&K into two Union Territories of Jammu & Kashmir and Ladakh, the leaders of the NC argued that the legislation approved by the Parliament and the orders issued by the President subsequently were 'unconstitutional' and prayed for these to be declared as 'void and inoperative'.

The petitioners further submitted that the legislation and the Presidential Orders are 'illegal and violative' of fundamental rights guaranteed under Article 14 and 21 of the Constitution to the people of Jammu and Kashmir. The two MPs submitted that the apex court has to examine whether the Union government can 'unilaterally' unravel the unique federal scheme under the cover of President's Rule while undermining crucial elements of due process and rule of law. 'This case, therefore, goes to the heart of Indian federalism, democratic processes and the rule of the apex court as the guardian of the federal structure,' the petition said. They submitted that Article 370 was extensively considered as carefully drafted in order to ensure the peaceful and democratic accession of the former princely state of Jammu and Kashmir to the Indian Union.

The two parliamentarians further contended that the Presidential Orders and the new legislation 'unconstitutionally undermine the scheme of Article 370. The first Presidential Order uses Article 370 (1)(d)—this was meant to apply other provisions of the Constitution to Jammu and Kashmir—to alter Article 370 itself and thereby the terms of federal relationship between J&K and Union of India', they submitted.

Several people and political parties have filed petitions before the apex court on various issues including some similar to the aforementioned ones.

A five-judge Constitution Bench headed by Justice N.V. Ramana and comprising Justices S.K. Kaul, R. Subhash Reddy, B.R. Gavai and Surya Kant has commenced hearings on a batch of petitions on the aforesaid issues.

***

This is the broad presentation on the facts, events, legislative provisions, etc., related to the birth of Article 370, its continuance for about 69 years of existence, much diluted over the years though, and then the recent Government actions of 5 and 6 August 2019, regarding abrogation of the special status given to the State of Jammu & Kashmir.

The basic purpose of this monograph is to make the Common Man more informed about the events and issues. Meanwhile the bifurcation of the State of Jammu & Kashmir and Ladakh has taken effect on 31 October 2019. The Lt. Governors of the two Union Territories have taken over their charges. Legislative restructuring is a work in progress, with a lot remaining to be done. While 153 state laws are to be repealed, 166 have been retained. Then there is the exercise of repealing Acts that mention 'applicable to all of India but not the state of Jammu and Kashmir'.

As of now, the state administration has implemented all that is mentioned in the Reorganisation Act as it is. But it is also saddled with the massive legislative exercise of arriving at and making state-specific insertions into the 108 Central laws that would now be applicable to the two new Union Territories. Another question is how will the assets be shared? There will be some more administrative issues too.

Be that as it may, as of now the Jury is still out! Our wait to hear the last word from the Supreme Court on various issues explained in these pages has thus begun.

References

Akbar, M.J. 1991. *Kashmir behind the Vale*. New Delhi: Viking.

Basu, Durga Das. 1997. *Introduction to the Constitution of India*. New Delhi: Prentice-Hall of India.

Dogra, Rajiv. 2015. *Where Borders Bleed*. New Delhi: Rupa.

Guha, Ramachandra. 2008. *India After Gandhi: The History of the World's Largest Democracy*. New Delhi: Picador.

Jagmohan. 1994. *My Frozen Turbulence in Kashmir*. New Delhi: Allied Publishers.

Jha, Prem Shankar. 1996. *Kashmir, 1947–Rival Versions of History*. New Delhi: Oxford University Press.

Korbel, Josef. 1954. *Danger in Kashmir*. Princeton: Princeton University Press.

Lamb, Alastair. 1992. *Kashmir—A Disputed legacy 1846-1990*. Karachi: Oxford University Press.

Mahajan, Mehr Chand. 1963. *Looking Back*. New Delhi: Asia Publishing House

Noorani, A.G. 2014. .*Article 370: A Constitutional History of Jammu and Kashmir*. New Delhi: Oxford University Press.

Sankaranarayanan, Gopal. 2016. *The Constitution of India*. New Delhi: National Law University.

Soz, Saifuddin. 2018. *Kashmir—Glimpses of History and the Story of Struggle*. New Delhi: Rupa.

Thomas, Raju G.C., ed. 1992. *Perspectives on Kashmir—The Roots of Conflict in South Asia*. USA: Westview.

Acknowledgements

In writing this book in a short span of time, I have received help of different kinds from many friends and relations in various ways. I acknowledge their help and thank them. They include K.M. Chandrasekhar, Ambassador Rajiv Dogra, Susmita Jha, Bhaswati Datta, Suchandra Ghosh, Susmita Gupta, Hemangini Dutt Majumder, Kajal Singh, Shobha John, Kalyani Gokhale, Rishi Majumder, Jayanta Roy Choudhury, Najib Shah, Upendra Singh Yadav, Ambassador T.C.A. Raghavan, Ambassador Asoke Mukerji, Prof. Sunil Mani, Prof Biswajit Dhar, A.K. Raha, S.K. Chaudhury, Anol Nath Chatterji, Amitava Roy, Somesh Arora, Rakesh Chitkara, Ramesh Ramchandra, Shailendra Kumar, B.B. Mohapatra, Gautam Chaudhury, Deepankar Aron, Abhik Gupta, Rahul Gokhale, J.P. Banerji, Partha Sengupta, Shyam K. Mahanta, Debojyoti Ghosh, Dr Kamal Bose, Dr Amit Mitra, Jawhar Sircar, Vijay Yadav, Samar Jha, Partha Bhattacharya and R.K. Jain.

Finally, I thank the Publishers Niyogi Books, in general, and Nirmal Kanti Bhattacharya, the man behind this effort of mine, Bikash De Niyogi, Tultul De Niyogi, Trisha De Niyogi, K.E. Priyamvada and Avik Goswami in particular, for bringing out this book on priority.

Index

About the Author

Sumit Dutt Majumder, former Chairman, Central Board of Excise and Customs, joined the Indian Revenue Service in 1974, after his Masters in Physics from IIT, Kharagpur. In the course of his career, he had dealt with various legal and constitutional issues and thus he is conversant with the nuances of the Constitution. On the GST Constitution Amendment Bill, he presented his views to the Select Committee of the Rajya Sabha in 2015. He is the author of *Customs Valuation Law and Practice* and four books on GST, the latest one being *GST Explained for the Common Man*. He can be reached at sumitduttmajumder@gmail.com.

www.ingramcontent.com/pod-product-compliance
Lightning Source LLC
Chambersburg PA
CBHW051440130726
47987CB00005B/2126